THE FACTORY

HIROKO OYAMADA
THE FACTORY

translated from the Japanese
by David Boyd

A NEW DIRECTIONS
PAPERBOOK ORIGINAL

The Factory was originally published in 2013 as *Kojo* by Shinchosha
Publishing Co., Tokyo. This English edition is published by arrangement
with Shinchosha Publishing Co. in care of Tuttle-Mori Agency, Inc., Tokyo.

The translator would like to thank Hitomi Olson for her generous assistance.

First published as New Directions Paperbook 1460 in 2019
Manufactured in the United States of America
New Directions Books are printed on acid-free paper
Design by Erik Rieselbach

Library of Congress Cataloging-in-Publication Data
Names: Oyamada, Hiroko, 1983– author. | Boyd, David (David G.), translator.
Title: The factory / by Hiroko Oyamada ; translated by David Boyd.
Other titles: Kojo. English
Description: New Direction Books : New York, 2019.
Identifiers: LCCN 2019020096 | ISBN 9780811228855 (alk. paper)
Classification: LCC PL874.Y36 K6513 2019 | DDC 895.63/6—dc23
LC record available at https://lccn.loc.gov/2019020096

10 9

New Directions Books are published for James Laughlin
by New Directions Publishing Corporation
80 Eighth Avenue, New York 10011

THE FACTORY

AS I OPENED THE BASEMENT-LEVEL DOOR, I THOUGHT I could smell birds. "Hello, I'm here for a two o'clock interview," I said to the overweight woman seated under a sign that read PRINT SERVICES RECEPTION. Without looking up, she nodded and lifted the receiver. I watched her mouth the words, *Your two o'clock is here.* Her lipstick had come off in places. "He'll be right with you," she said—and suddenly there he was right in front of me, a middle-aged man with a ragged, rectangular face. I immediately recognized what he had in his hand: my application packet. "Welcome to the Print Services Branch Office," he said, "I'm Goto, thanks for coming." "Thank you, I'm Ushiyama," I replied. His face was red and his eyes were clouded—the whites were almost yellow, obscuring the boundaries of his irises. Maybe he was drunk. Or maybe this was just how overworked middle managers looked, devoid of life and spirit.

Goto led me to what he called the conference room, which wasn't actually a room at all. It was more like a partitioned space, near the door and facing the reception desk. He directed me toward a black leather two-seater and I placed the leatherette bag that I always bring to interviews on the cushion next to me. "I'm Yoshiko Ushiyama, thank you for meeting with me," I reiterated. The noise from the basement was sinking in now. But it wasn't the talking or the ringing phones. It was the constant buzz and hum of the machines. "The pleasure's mine, and please make yourself comfortable, I hope you don't mind if I review your application while we speak," he said, reading off the cover: "First name: Yoshiko. Last name: Ushiyama. Now there's a name you don't see very often. Though I guess there was Mei Ushiyama. Ever heard of her?" "No, I don't think so." Then Goto started to count: "One, two . . . and this makes six." I knew what he was getting at. Since graduating, I'd quit five companies. This job would be my sixth. The Education and Work Experience sections of my application spilled into the margins. I'd also attached a separate History of Employment that ran three pages. From my start and end dates, he could see that I hadn't held onto any job for more than a year. I left most of them after about six months. "Please allow me to explain . . ." "I know, it didn't work out. It's that simple. Sometimes things click, sometimes they don't. Sometimes you can't make things happen, no matter how hard you try. Trust me, I've seen it all . . . Anyway, how about you start by telling me about yourself and why you think you'd be right for this position." "Of course, well, I was a liberal arts major at university, where my research focused on the Japanese language. Specifically, I'm interested in how people communicate. While pursuing my research, I became curious about the use of language in print media. I was especially fascinated by the effectiveness of particular expressions and sentence structures. Ideally, I'd like to work in a field that allows me to utilize this background. That's what led me to apply for this position. I remember being a girl and seeing TV commercials and newspaper ads for the products made here. I was drawn to the idea of working at this company because of its famously high standards, both technologically and ethically speaking . . ." "Yes," he said, "yes."

This wasn't my first time at the factory. I'd come on a field trip when I was in elementary school. A woman in a tiny stewardess hat showed us around the museum and gave us a tour of the factory floor. I went home that day with a box of souvenirs that had a photo of the factory printed on the lid. Inside was a fabric pencil case with a two-color retractable pen and a set of mechanical pencils, as well as a box of cookies that were shaped like dictionaries, race cars, and seashells. Other kids got different shapes. Houses, towers, dinosaurs, and faces. At the time, it felt like the factory was enormous, maybe as big as Disneyland. And the souvenirs were as good as Disneyland's, too. On the walk from the parking lot to the factory, we saw adults dressed in all kinds of clothes: suits, coveralls, lab coats. Walking among them, I caught glimpses of the factory buildings, but couldn't see anything beyond that. No matter where you are in this city—the school, the department store, anywhere—you're always walled in by mountains. But the factory had nothing around it. Or rather, it was as if it were surrounded by something other than the mountains. Something larger, something more distant.

Seeing the factory again as an adult, it didn't feel any smaller. If anything, it had gotten even bigger. The factory's influence over the city was too great to ignore. Everyone has at least one family member working for the factory, or one of its partners or subsidiaries. Vans and trucks with its logos can be seen on every street, and ambitious parents start nudging their kids toward a factory career even before they can read. My parents weren't like that, but when my brother graduated from university, he landed a job at one of the factory's offices in the heart of the city, doing computer work all day. It was almost strange how I'd managed to go through five jobs here without ever working for them. Maybe it looked like I was avoiding the factory, but I really wasn't. I'd always seen the factory in a positive light, ever since that childhood field trip. If anything, I thought, maybe unconsciously, that I didn't deserve to work somewhere so important. Yet here I was at the factory for the second time in my life, being interviewed. Goto held in his hands the application that I'd mailed off with no expectation of an answer. It had been my brother's idea. He'd told me that I didn't need to worry about chipping in on living expenses, but apparently he hadn't given up on me finding a real job. He tossed the ad in my lap and said, "Yoshiko, you should apply for this. It's a permanent position, at the factory. All you need is a four-year degree."

Goto listened patiently as I explained why I had left each of my five previous jobs. In every case, I admitted, some of the blame was mine, but of course my former employers had also played a role in my premature departures. Goto occasionally threw in a supportive *I see* or *Uh-huh*. Then another overweight woman walked in—this one's lipstick was impeccable—and said, "Goto-saaan, city council, line three." This, I thought, is why interviews should be conducted in private rooms, to avoid unnecessary interruptions. Goto turned to me and said, "Hold that thought," then he got up to take the call. I suppose he didn't have a choice. It was the city council, after all.

"Now, Ushiyama-san," Goto began again, returning from the call, "How would you feel about coming on as a contract employee? It's a different listing. One second, I'll print it out for you ..." I didn't know what to say. In that moment, I felt like I'd been tricked. But then I started to feel something else, something like relief—it was as if the world made sense again. The permanent position was too good to be true, a liberal arts degree couldn't get you a permanent job in a place like this, and I obviously wasn't the sort of applicant that companies would go out of their way to hire, especially not at this stage in my career. Goto had been really kind to me, too. All the interview manuals I'd read advised that when the interviewer is being too nice, it's a clear sign that you're not getting the job, or at least that the conditions won't be the same as advertised. And that was exactly what was happening.

"You'd still work here in Print Services, but as part of the Staff

Support team. They're currently hiring contract employees. On the bright side, with this position, you can pick your own hours, and the work won't be very demanding. This honestly seems like the best fit for you, considering your employment history. We'll take it from there. If that sounds good, I'll bring you down to Staff Support and introduce you to the team. They're down at the far end of the corridor."

The far end of the corridor had an ominous sound to it, like the place was reserved for dead-end employees. Goto handed me a printout of the new job description. Some of the details were exactly the same as the permanent position, others weren't. For one, permanent employees had to have at least a BA, but there were no educational requirements for this position. A permanent post meant a fixed monthly salary, but the contract job was hourly. Work hours were different, too. Permanent employees work Monday through Friday, 9 a.m. to 5:30 p.m. (flextime available), but this job was for 3 to 7.5 hours daily (at least two days a week), somewhere between the hours of 9 and 5:30. I couldn't figure out the difference between a monthly salary and hourly pay, at least not on the spot, but I was confident that the latter wouldn't be as good. Part of me felt undervalued, but they must have seen some promise in me. I mean, they were still offering me a job. In a way, this made things easier. Goto and I were, in fact, much closer to arriving at a decision. If I were being considered for the other position, the interview would end, then I'd say goodbye and head home. Goto would look over my application, and a few days later they would contact me if I'd made it to the next round. If they'd decided to move forward, there might be a second interview or some test. But with this new contract job, the only question was how I felt about the description that Goto had placed in front of me. It really wasn't complicated. I only had to decide whether I would give in or hold out. But could you even call that giving in? In times like these, a job's a job, even if it pays by the hour, even if it isn't permanent, even if it's physical labor. This wasn't a bad thing. On the contrary, it could be the best thing for me.

"Specifically, what kind of work would I be handling?" "Support." At that point, I'd assumed that *support* meant something like unpacking reams of paper and loading them into the printers, or replacing dead toner cartridges.

The job they assigned me was document destruction: operating a shredder all day, as a member of what they called the Shredder Squad. We were stationed at the far end of the basement floor, in a room stocked with machines made for destroying large quantities of paper. That was going to be my job—for up to 7.5 hours per day.

AT FIRST, I THOUGHT THE BLACK BIRDS WERE CROWS, BUT I was mistaken. They had to be closer to cormorants, maybe shags. Gathered by the edge of the water, far from where I was standing on the bridge, I could see some of them, clumped together, staring at the factory. They looked slick as oil, like if you wrung one by the neck you'd get black ink all over your hands. They were floating in brackish water, where the river spills into the ocean. But do shags live in places like that? Are they ocean birds? River birds? I wiped the sweat from my forehead.

It was almost evening. After stopping at several sites along the way, the orientation hike—a training and networking event for new hires—was wrapping up for the day. We were close to the factory's south side now, on a large bridge that stretches over the river separating the north and south zones. The bridge has two lanes of car traffic flanked by wide footpaths. In the time it took our group to cross, we saw at least five buses, three excavators with their shovels tucked downward like the heads of sleeping giraffes, one concrete mixer, five vehicles loaded with some kind of heavy equipment, and too many cars to count. Maybe half of them were company cars. Gray, with the factory logo on the side. There were a few jeeps, too. "This bridge feels sturdy, doesn't it? Even with this wind, and all the buses, it doesn't wobble," said the young man walking next to me, a gifted soul with a knack for communication, hired by the factory straight out of school (no easy feat, to be sure). He was refreshingly self-assured, and when I was quiet for too long he'd try to make conversation. Still, he was more interested in the group to his other side, two men and three women, among whom he had already established himself as the leader of the pack. And what a leader he was, refusing to let the silent, brooding types peel away from the group. Can't blame him for trying. I wonder if he knows I'm ten years older than he is. I was late to join the workforce, but I don't look my age—probably because I've never had to live through the horrors of job hunting. I'm well aware of how young I look, but I still can't believe I'm here, walking around with these kids as if I were one of them. It was never something I wanted. Even now, it feels like someone's playing a trick on me. But why? Who could possibly benefit from that? I kept on walking. "You're from around here, aren't you? We were thinking about going out after the hike. Any places you'd recommend? You're welcome to join us, by the way." I guess that means he's not from around here. The finest applicants from all across Japan are dying to work at this factory. I never saw the appeal. Maybe the factory is generous with funding? Granted, a top-tier corporation would be much better funded than some provincial university, but what difference does it make if you can't do what you want? "Actually, my university's up by the mountains. It's not around here. And, I'm sorry to say, I have plans tonight." I really did. Some guys from school, the elite few who'd managed to land jobs in the area, were throwing me a party.

"Look at you, Furufue. From researcher to corporate scientist, just like that. Looks like you hit the jackpot," they'd said, acting like I'd won some huge victory by getting this job. They thought I was lucky, but I didn't see it that way. This whole situation was nothing but a pain. Honestly, I would've rather continued my research at the university. "Taxonomy isn't exactly a growing field, you know. Genetics, now that's another story. But what do you do? You classify moss. That just makes you weird. Following a path this narrow doesn't leave you with many options. No one wants you to get stuck down some dead-end path. I know I don't. Your parents can't look after you forever, can they? Your dad may have some influence, but there's no guarantee that something's going to open up for you at the school, no matter how long you hang around. Things just don't work that way." Out of nowhere, my advisor came and asked me if I'd like to get something to eat in the cafeteria. It was ten in the morning and I'd just arrived at the lab. It was too late for breakfast, but too early for lunch. I had to order something, so I went with a bowl of miso soup—the one with no pork—and paid my thirty yen. I walked over to the tea dispenser, poured two cups of hojicha, then carried them over to our table. My advisor was already sitting. In front of him was a giant slab of tonkatsu, stir-fried eggplant and pork liver, an extra-large helping of rice, natto, and seven umeboshi from the condiment island. "Did I tell you about my diet? I've been skipping lunch. I stick to two meals a day, no carbs at night. I lost over twenty pounds in the past six months." Around that time, whenever he had something to drink or something sweet to eat, in fact any time he put anything in his mouth, he'd given the exact same speech. Everyone in the lab, myself included, had already committed the whole routine to memory. Admittedly, I hadn't seen him eat rice or noodles at night, but I'd seen him knock back more than a few carb-heavy beers, and he never turned down fried food. Look at him—eating that many umeboshi is too much salt for anyone. As he poured most of his stir-fry over his rice and started digging in, he told me about the factory job. "The offer came through the placement office. They need a bryologist. The office asked me if anybody came to mind and I gave them your name." After shoveling the stir-fry and rice into his mouth and slurping it down, he got back up to put some Thousand Island dressing on the shredded cabbage that came with his tonkatsu. I was lost. They need a bryologist? My advisor returned to his seat and resumed eating. "It's not a bad gig, this job. You should really think about it." "Does the factory have some particular interest in moss?" "No clue. They mentioned something about green-roofing, though. You should go over to the placement office and see what the description says." He took the cabbage off his plate, pink with dressing, put it on his rice, then crammed it into his mouth. Setting his chopsticks down for a moment, he stuck an umeboshi in his mouth, sucked off the flesh, cracked the stone with his molars, and tongued free the innermost kernel before spitting it back onto his plate. "Green-roofing? They should ask a specialist. These days, all you need to do is lay down some sheet, then add water . . ." I looked at my soup. All the ingredients had settled on the bottom. I didn't bother eating any. Then I watched my advisor cover his natto in mustard, pour some soy sauce on top, and dump the whole thing over the last of his rice. I remembered him once saying how much he loved the taste of natto with mayonnaise. I bet the only reason he was holding back now was because the cafeteria charges ten yen per packet. Diet? What bullshit. "I don't know what to tell you, Furufue. This is a job in the factory—we're talking big leagues here. What more do you need to know?" he asked, thick strings of natto webbing his mouth. I had a rough idea where the factory was. I knew some of their products, too. I'd even used a few. But why would they need me? It didn't make sense. "To be honest, I'm not sure I'm ready to leave the program. Isn't there anyone else?" "No," he shot back, using his chopsticks to slice through his natto. "Furufue, buddy. The factory went out of their way to ask our university for someone. If we recommend the wrong person, it'll negatively impact our placements in the future. We need to give them our best and brightest. That's why it has to be you. Besides, they're asking for a bryologist ..." He poured some tea into his bowl, started stirring with his chopsticks, brought it to his mouth, and washed down the natto stuck between his teeth. He inhaled another umeboshi while I thought of at least two talented researchers who were more deserving of this post. It's not like I thought I wasn't a good enough candidate, but they were older and more qualified. I couldn't think of one good reason why I should get this job instead of them. I was about to say as much, too, but my advisor spoke first. "Just consider it. Think about how happy it'll make your folks." And that was the end of that.

My parents really were overjoyed. Here I'd thought they were perfectly content with my decision to devote myself to research, even if it meant I couldn't make much money. Apparently, I was wrong: "A man's mission in life is to make his own way in the world." It didn't seem like much of a mission to me, but my father issued that decree over the dinner table while my mother used her napkin to wipe away the tears of joy. The next day, the three of us went suit shopping. "It doesn't matter if you're over thirty, you're just getting started. You don't want to make the wrong impression by wearing something too nice." The suits my father picked out were apparently just right. "You actually look pretty good in a suit," he said. I thought we were going to get a single suit for the interview and leave it at that, but my father, full of pride now that his son was finally going to work, grabbed ten neckties and shirts, a couple of gray suits, one in navy, and another in black that I could wear to formal events—meanwhile, my mother tracked down ten pairs of socks and ten handker-chiefs. "Don't touch the summerwear until you're hired. This should do it for now. You're lucky, you know. Most interview-ees have to do this shopping in the worst heat, over the summer of their third year. Okay, let's get you some shoes ..." My father addressed the white-haired clerk and told him to hold onto my measurements. At the shoe shop, we bought two pairs while my father said, "Let's admit it. You're an introvert. You're no good with people. I figured you'd never voluntarily work as part of a team, but this is a real stroke of luck. You better thank your advisor. The factory, too. Be grateful! Now listen, if anything goes wrong, I want you to come straight to me. Don't complain to your coworkers, okay? If anything's off, you talk to me. We'll sort it out. Just don't try to do anything on your own. Most of all, remember to be thankful." Thankful for what?

"Hello, everybody. We're thrilled to have you out here, joining us on this beautiful day. This is our tenth year running the hike. We offer this event to give you guys a chance to learn a little about the factory and your fellow new hires. My name is Goto, from the PR department, and I'll be your guide during the hike over the next two days. This is my first year in charge of the hike, but I've been with the factory for five years now, which means I'm not much older than the rest of you. So please don't hesitate to reach out. We have three more members from PR joining us today, helping out. Can I ask you to introduce yourselves?" Two young men and a woman bowed in near-perfect unison, smiles on their faces. "Hello, I'm Sakurai. This is my third year with the factory. It's nice to meet you." "I'm Ichihashi. It's my third year, too." "I'm Izumi Aoyama, originally from Hokkaido. This is my second year. Nice to meet you." Goto bowed back to them, then took over again. "There are fifty of us walking today, so we're going to go ahead and take attendance before we get moving. The order's a bit strange, based on when you applied for the hike and your department, so listen carefully. Be sure you raise your hand when you hear your name. Once you do, I want you to line up over here, in front of Aoyama-san. Okay, here we go. Furufue-san, Yoshio Furufue." What? Why me? "He—here," I said, my voice louder than I'd intended. Nonplussed, I cut through the crowd and stood in front of Aoyama, who smiled at me and said, "Nice to meet you." Why was I first? I signed up right before the deadline. Besides, my department, if I even had one, should have been last on the list. The Environmental Improvement Division Office for Green-Roof Research didn't even exist before I was hired. I was the entire department.

I went to HQ for the interview, or what I thought was going to be an interview. At the front desk, they told me where to wait. Inside, there was a conference table with a few chairs around it, but I decided to stand. I didn't want them to offer me the job. Really, I was better off without it, but I was still tense. Not long after I got there, someone came in and thanked me for coming in. "Did it take you long to get here? I'm Goto, from Public Relations. Nice to meet you," he said, holding out a business card and bowing. I had no card to offer in return, obviously, so I just bowed and introduced myself. "Okay, let's get right to it," he said, "You'll start on the first of April. In the three months between now and then, what we'd like from you is a list of necessary materials. Let us know as soon as you can . . ." What was he saying? "I'm terribly sorry, but I was under the impression I was here for an interview . . ." Goto's face was completely blank. "This isn't an interview. No one told me it was an interview. Besides, I'm not in charge of personnel. We're meeting today to discuss your responsibilities from April onward, and to make sure we have everything you'll need. I'm sure you'll need microscopes and things like that, won't you? We're going to need a list. Makes, models, part numbers, anything you can give us." Microscopes? "Will I be working with microscopes? I thought you needed an expert in bryology, to help you with green-roofing." What was I saying? I was just a researcher. I wasn't an expert in anything, not yet. "That's right, green-roofing. We have a few different organizations taking care of our trees, flowers, roads, and streetlights. Green-roofing has been a real blind spot, though, and that's why HQ finally decided to step in and deal with it on their own." "They made a new department?" "Correct. And when the factory decided moss would be the best way to go, we put in a call to your university," he said, blushing through a smile. I tried to piece together what I wanted to say. "When it comes to green-roofing, you'd be better off asking a specialist. These days, all you need to do is lay down a sheet and add water. The job would be finished in weeks. Well, considering how large the factory is, I suppose it could take a little longer. Anyway, my point is, there are businesses that specialize in that," I said. "Yes, we understand. As far as that goes, the factory generally frowns upon outsourcing. Almost everything here is handled by us or our subsidiaries. Likewise, as the EI Division Office for Green-Roof Research continues to develop, it could become its own subsidiary. We hope you'll work toward that goal." Its own subsidiary? "By the way, can I ask where you got your suit? It's very nice. Is it imported?" I had no idea. "Um, do you mind if I ask a question first? Is this going to be a team project? To be frank, going on without outside help could take a very, very long time. I'm afraid I don't see the merit in it, either. Forgive me if I'm overstepping, but ..." "No, yes, I understand. There's no need to worry about time. Please proceed at your own pace, whatever you think is feasible. There won't be anyone telling you to finish by a particular date or anything like that." And that's okay? Can they really afford to be so relaxed? Don't they realize how wasteful this is? "While my research has to do with moss, my interest is primarily taxonomical. Green-roofing requires cultivation knowledge. Will other bryologists be joining the office?" "For the time being, it'll just be you," he said, still smiling, although I thought I detected some pity in his eyes. His cheeks were as red as ever. "It's just me?" "That's correct." "One person? To get the whole thing going? And why is that?" Unbelievable. I really couldn't understand what he was saying, it was just too absurd. What idiot dreamed this up? "Well, yes. You see, that's why we aren't imposing any hard deadlines. Proceed at whatever pace suits you. We'd like for you to begin by collecting samples, moss samples, whatever pops up around the factory, and classifying what you find. In due course, we ask that you work toward greening. At any rate, classification comes first. Do you now see what we have in mind? Oh, here. This is going to be your badge. You'll need it whenever you enter or exit the factory. As long as you're on-site, we ask that you keep this on you at all times. See how the strap is silver? That gives you access to virtually anywhere on the premises. Needless to say, we don't want you wandering through the central buildings. When in doubt, be sure to set up an appointment beforehand. Anywhere outside is fine, wherever you need to go to find moss. We'll laminate the badge soon, but first we'll need to get your picture. It'll be ready for you on your first day of work, the first of April. Any questions?" "You mean you want me to green-roof the whole factory, on my own, without any real guidance or supervision? Would I go somewhere for training?" "Well, we offer a couple of basic training programs for new hires, one for etiquette and another for phone and email, but you won't be needing those. For starters, your position doesn't require much interaction with the outside world. And we have an orientation hike, equal parts training and networking for new hires." Orientation hike? "I'm sorry, I meant training in terms of cultivating moss, or green-roofing in general." "Training like that doesn't really exist. Vocational training tends to be OJT: on the job training. You learn as you go. Individual training is left up to individual sections, if not individual employees, and we'll sometimes have senior employees partner up with new hires, but there's really nothing beyond that." "In that case, how am I supposed to learn about the green-roofing process?" "Well, by utilizing your knowledge of moss. I know how this sounds, but we'll figure it out as you go." I just stared at Goto. I couldn't understand a word he was saying. No colleagues, maybe—but no supervisor? Now Goto was smiling even more radiantly than before. "Any other questions?"

"Okay, everyone. Please take a look at your maps. We're going to go over today's route. Right now, we're here, at the top. This is the north zone. We have our headquarters here, as well as the planning and design departments, which together serve as the main hub for the entire factory. The north gate, right here, is the main entrance to the factory, and this is where we'll start our hike today. We'll show you a few buildings on the east side, swing by a couple of shops, then arrive here at the main employee cafeteria for lunch, at around noon. You're in for a great meal, by the way, the new-hire special . . . Be sure to keep an eye on the time while we walk. If you show up after one o'clock, it'll mess everything up for the temp staff in charge of cleaning up. Okay? By the way, there are all kinds of other food options around the factory. We have nearly a hundred cafeterias, and a decent number of restaurants, too. If you want, mark your map as we go. To be honest, some places are much better than others. If you want to know about the best places to eat, I refer you to our own Aoyama-san. Ask her anything. Ehehehehe. Anyway, yes, after we have lunch, we'll keep heading south, toward the bottom of the map. We'll finish our day at the bridge, here. The southern area stretches out over the ocean. As you can see, this river divides the factory in two: the southwest and the northeast. The bridge that crosses the river, the central bridge, looks much larger in person than it does on the map. When you see it, you'll be blown away. Once we're over the bridge, we'll wrap up for the day. But we won't abandon you at the bridge, so don't worry. We'll get on the bus headed for the south gate, then part ways there. Once you exit the south gate, there's one bus bound for the station and another that heads into town. Everyone should be able to get home from there. If you're headed for the dorms, you can just hop on the factory shuttle. Tomorrow morning, we'll meet up at the south gate. Is that clear? Does anyone have any questions?" No one raised their hands. Looking down at my map, I was overwhelmed. The factory was a world of its own. Only four ways in and out. North, South, East, West. Shouldn't there be more? Next to the roads on the map were colorful circles—blue, green, and orange—and according to the legend in the corner these indicated bus stops: there were several bus lines, running through the factory, all day long. Three giant buildings loomed over the rest: the factory headquarters, the museum, and the main warehouse. The rest of the map was filled with smaller buildings, all roughly the same size, too numerous to count. There were also a few areas marked "Residential," and an enormous lot labeled "Product Test Site." "Okay then. I'll start by talking about where we are now, the north zone. Many people who come to the north zone, including our business partners and visitors, have never been to the factory before, and many of them will never come again. Most high-ranking employees have offices in the north zone. In that sense, this is a very important sector, where the factory presents itself to the world. Some of you are going to be working here in the north zone, and some of you won't. Whatever the case, when you're here, be sure you're always dressed your best. It's important that we do everything we can to preserve the factory's image. Appearance matters."

In the middle of what I thought was going to be my interview with Goto, I got up to go to the restroom. There was a window right in front of the toilet. It was the sort of window you open by releasing the latch and pushing outward while turning the handle. I wanted a little fresh air. As I went to open it, a sign posted over the faded wallpaper caught my attention: KEEP WINDOW CLOSED: BIRDS IN AREA. "Okay, what am I supposed to do first?" The first thing they asked me to do was run a moss hunt. "A what?" "A moss hunt. You know—a hunt, for moss."

I REALIZED IT AS SOON AS I OPENED MY EYES. I THOUGHT I'd been reading, reading something indecipherable, but I was actually sleeping. As soon as I started feeling tired, I was asleep. Dreaming. I could see shadowy black shapes, even now. I looked around, but I was positive no one had noticed. The partitions made sure of that. As long as someone wasn't looking into my area from directly behind me, there was no way anyone could have seen me. But even if they hadn't, the whole thing set me on edge. I'd always thought sleeping on the job was a sign of laziness. If you're feeling tired, you can always stand up, go to the bathroom, rinse your mouth out with water or wash your hands, really scrub them. If it's particularly bad, you can wash your face or even use a couple of eyedrops. That had always done the trick before, not that I usually got tired at work. I almost never did, unless I had to stay up late the night before. That only happened when I was swamped. My whole life I'd thought that people who drifted off at work were just a bunch of slackers. But now I was that slacker. Only I wasn't slacking. I'd gone to sleep early the night before. The thing was, the moment I started feeling even remotely tired, that was the end of it, I was gone, but obviously I didn't notice until I woke up again. When did I fall asleep? How long was I out? I know I'd been reading. Then I was half asleep, then asleep. I must have really passed out. And I thought I had it covered. It was the partitions. Hidden from my coworkers, I let my guard down. I was sweating a little, clutching my printout. The red pen in my other hand had run wild while I slept, leaving jagged lines all over the page. "Crap," I muttered, then looked around again. It didn't seem like Kasumi had heard. The room was silent as ever. Irinoi and Glasses were working quietly. Or maybe they were sleeping, too. How would I even know? The makeshift walls between us had ensured a new level of privacy. I looked at the printout again and got back to work.

I'd heard about the crows, the beavers, and the other animals around the factory, but hadn't seen much of anything myself. Really, I was just happy to have a place to work, a place to go every day. Then again, that relief was not without some sadness. I'd switched jobs, and before I'd even fallen into the rhythm of the new job it was abundantly clear that there would be no need to worry, that it was going to be easy. The work was no big deal. Once that sank in, I realized: I'm a temp worker. Until recently, very recently, I'd been a systems engineer for a small company, when, out of nowhere, everything changed. "Fired?" "Sorry to say it, but yes." If my girlfriend hadn't been working as a coordinator for a temp agency, I'd be out of work right now. Unemployed at thirty, going on thirty-one. Instead I'm doing this work that literally anyone could do, as if nothing I'd ever done in my life even mattered. But how could I complain? Having work beats not having work. That goes without saying. Unemployment is hell. Temp work, though? Thanks to my girlfriend, I landed a place in the factory's Document Division, proofreading printouts by hand. My life had always revolved around computers, and now I wasn't even using one.

"We already have one temp in the office, and they asked us for one more. It'll be the perfect fit for you! I'm so glad they weren't looking for a receptionist or something. Talk about great timing!" I can only imagine how deflated I looked, but my girlfriend was being unreasonably cheerful, tossing her hair back repeatedly. She'd just cut it shorter than it'd been in years, and it seemed like she was really enjoying the way her hair felt against her cheeks and the back of her neck. Tossing her hair around like that made her look like an idiot. But this idiot turned out to be my sole lifeline. "Don't worry. Just leave it to me." In the morning, the first thing I'd do was grab a packet and remove the paper inside. I'd read it over, looking for errors, making notes as I went. This is the job I was given: "It's best to go into this assuming everyone makes mistakes. In reality, that's not how it works. Still, when you find something wrong, leave a note in the margins. Like this. There are marks you're supposed to use, which are all in this handbook. Look up the right mark, then use that. Except, well, it's an old system, invented back when we did everything by hand. Feel free to do whatever works for you. You graduated from college, so I'm sure your Japanese is in good shape." My first day on the job, the middle-aged man in charge of the department showed me to my empty desk—no computer, nothing. Depressing. He handed me a gray sleeve protector, a Japanese dictionary, an English-Japanese dictionary, a character dictionary, and the proofreader's handbook. After he'd shown me around most of the floor, the man said, "If there's anything else you want to know, you can ask anyone here." Then he ran off. By *anyone here*, he meant the three other proofreaders. All temps, but only one from my girlfriend's agency. The other two came from somewhere else. The man left without bothering to introduce us, so I took matters into my own hands. "Hello," I said. The women from the other agency just looked at me, but the one from my girlfriend's agency, Kasumi (I could see KASUMI written in all caps on the ID hanging around her neck), said hello back, bowing slightly. "You're the coordinator's boyfriend, aren't you? That's what I heard," she whispered. She smelled like peaches. Her lips were glistening and she had kind wrinkles under her eyes. Was she older than she looked?

"Good for you. She's a real catch," she said, still whispering, but I could tell the other women were listening to every single word, grinning at each other. "Sorry? No, it's not like that. Did she say that?" "Uh-huh." Gossip already. Why did my girlfriend have to tell her about us? Doesn't she know how that looks? They're going to think I can't get a job on my own. I know she's a permanent employee for a well-known agency, but she's really not that bright. To be honest, all she does is assign temps to posts, which is hardly a skilled profession.

"Okay, let's go over what you'll be doing. First, grab one of the packets over here, whichever you like. You're going to be checking what's inside. If you need more pens or Post-its, you can find them on the shelf right there." Kasumi then showed me the contents of the packet that was open on her own desk. It was a side-stitched book and a stack of maybe thirty sheets of A3 paper. There were other packets, lots of them, exactly like this one, filed in a cabinet that stood as high as my chest. On the front of each packet was a date and some kind of code, a combination of letters and numbers. Next to that was a space for the supervisor to sign or stamp. I grabbed a handful of packets to take a look. As far as I could tell, they weren't in any particular order. Some had today's date while others were from ten years ago. The names in the supervisor box were all new to me. None had been signed by the middle-aged man or Kasumi. Just like Kasumi said, our job was to take whatever we found in the packets—documents of various types and formats—and proof them. In some files, there were additional materials, like manuscripts or newspaper articles. If that was the case, we were supposed to check the document against them for accuracy. When there was nothing else inside, just the one document, we were supposed to use our dictionaries, consult the proofing manual, and correct the Japanese accordingly. "Then, when you're finished with everything in the packet, you shelve it over there. Once a day, these files are collected." "So we don't have to sign them or anything?" "Sign them?" "You know, to prove you checked it." "Haha, that won't be necessary, no," Kasumi said, waving her hand in front of her face like the thought had never crossed her mind. "Ushiyama-san, you're pretty serious, aren't you?" Now she smelled like pineapple candy. She spoke quietly, like before, but the other two women were definitely listening. I could feel them looking at us, then at each other, smirking. One was middle-aged with a brownish perm, the other was younger with blue glasses. I wouldn't call them ugly, but they weren't exactly memorable. Their attitudes weren't that great, either. Kasumi was a little on the heavy side, but she was, without a doubt, the most likeable of the three. She almost looked like a preschool teacher. It was good we were from the same agency. I remembered my girlfriend saying Kasumi was like an aunt. That crossed a line, though. It's not about your age, but your mental state, and Kasumi felt more like an older sister than an aunt. "If you don't put your name on it, how do they keep track of who's responsible for what? What if you made some huge mistake?" Why shouldn't I take this seriously? I don't want to make mistakes. I don't want to cause any problems. What's wrong with that? Kasumi grinned, saying, "You won't make any mistakes. You can't." "What do you mean?" "You'll see. We proof everything and leave notes, right? So, you do that, send it out, wait a while, and eventually the same thing comes back. Another version of the same document. Sometimes, though, it's even worse than before. It just makes you ask yourself, what have I been doing? Someone somewhere is probably doing something with our edits, but we don't even know who. Once in a while, you'll fill a whole page with red marks, but it's not like you're really changing the content or anything. You'll see what I mean. Sometimes you find a typo, a misspelling, or an unindented paragraph. Nothing you'll find is all that major to begin with, so if you miss something, it's no big deal." "You still need to correct everything, though," said the temp with the perm, looking right at us. We'd been speaking so quietly that I couldn't believe she'd heard what we'd said. "You don't have to sign anything. If anything happens, though, it's everyone's fault, so don't screw up." Kasumi nodded, then turned to me. "Like she said, okay? If anything comes up, you can use the phone over there to call the manager. Want some?" She held out a couple pieces of red candy with twisted wrappers. The color matched her nails perfectly. I said thanks, took one, unwrapped it, and popped it in my mouth. I bit into the hard shell and soft chocolate filled my mouth. It was time to start, so I grabbed a packet and pulled out what was inside.

Goodbye to All Your Problems and Mine: A Guide to Mental Health Care. It was a thin B4-size booklet. Beneath its excremental title was a drawing of two smiling meatballs, basking under a rainbow. On the next sheet was a two-page spread with wide margins, presumably to give us more space for feedback. The cover looked okay, so I moved on to the table of contents. What the hell was this? From the second chapter onward, every chapter was listed as starting on page seventeen. The leader dots running between the chapter titles and page numbers were a mess, too. I crossed them out, then wrote in the correct numbers. As long as you gave them a decent explanation, it was the sort of job even a middle-schooler could handle. Isn't there something else I could be doing? Something a little more up my alley? I mean, these days, you really have to go out of your way to find a job that has nothing to do with computers. In this economy, it's unbelievable that the factory was still willing to add new proofreaders to their payroll, even as temps. Anyway, even if it wasn't a perfect fit, I had to count my blessings. It wasn't even physical labor—and it was a whole lot easier than working at some convenience store. I should probably be grateful that I can take home 150,000 yen a month doing this. Still, the second the economy turns around,

I'll find something else. I'd thought about asking my girlfriend to find me something where I could use my expertise, but it'd just be another temp job anyway. Why bother? I'd rather be fully employed. Obviously. I wanted to get married at some point. I had my sister to think about, too. She had her contract job, but who knows how long that would last?

I DIDN'T WANT HIM ASKING WHAT KIND OF WORK IT WAS. I didn't want to tell him. Fortunately, when I said I was going to be a contract worker at the factory, he didn't bother asking anything else. He just gave me this look like I should probably report them to the Labor Standards Bureau. I told him I'd be going to work five days a week, starting Monday. "It's full-time, though?" he asked, then told me to calculate my monthly rate. "They'll cover your commute, right?" They would, apparently.

The interview ended and Goto walked me over to the shredder station. It was also in the basement, but farther back. The Print Services Branch Office was a long rectangle with doors on the north and south walls, both of which led to the stairs. On the other side of the door to the north was the reception desk and the space where I'd had my interview. On that side of the floor were three islands made up of six desks each. The people there were talking and phones were ringing. The rest of the floor belonged to the printing station. We were surrounded by printers, copiers, cutters, folding machines, devices of all shapes and sizes. As we walked by, Goto pointed around, telling me what each one did, even though most of them were too obvious to need any explanation. In the middle of the area was a giant worktable. The men and women around the table were wearing jumpsuits and gray aprons. The smell of ink and oil filled the air. The noise from the machines was so constant it almost felt quiet. I guess I'd already gotten used to it. One wall was hidden behind shelves stacked to the ceiling with paper, toner, and machine parts. At a break in those shelves was the shredder station. "This is Staff Support. Just like home, don't you think? It's usually pretty quiet. How many people are here? Not many . . . Just like home," Goto said, coming to a stop. By the south door, where it's darker than the rest of the floor, I could see fourteen shredders, but only a few aproned employees using the machines—it almost looked like they were underwater, like they were moving slower than the rest of us. I wanted to count them, but stopped shy of really doing it. The shredders were set up against the walls in two rows of seven. Ten of them were standard sized, but four were much larger. Goto saw me eyeing the shredder station. "Technically, I'm in charge of Staff Support, but your team has its own captain. He's in the hospital right now, but he'll be back soon. Maybe in two weeks? Definitely before the month's up. For now, you can talk to me about your schedule. You can find me right over here. If you have any questions about your duties, please talk to the woman over there, Itsumi-san. Hey, Itsumi-san, can I borrow you for a minute?" The woman Goto called over was tiny, with unnaturally straight black hair tied up in a ponytail and Coke-bottle glasses. "This is Ushiyama-san. She'll be joining us here, starting next week. She's a contract worker, but she's elected to work Monday through Friday, 9 to 5:30. Could I ask you to show her the ropes?" "Absolutely. I'd be happy to," she squeaked. "We'll have your apron and ID badge ready before you start. Itsumi-san will hold onto them for you, okay?" I could feel Goto looking at me. "It's nice to meet you. I'm Yoshiko Ushiyama," I said to the girl, bowing slightly. As she nodded back to me, I spotted a few gray hairs. "I'm Itsumi. It's really nice to meet you." Her gold-framed glasses had vine-like patterns running along the temples. "When you come to the factory on your first day, you won't have your badge yet, so they won't let you past the gate. When you get there, have them call me, okay? Goto, at the Print Services Branch Office." Yeah, I know the routine. That's what I did today. "Right, one more thing. From now on, there's no need to dress up. As a rule, our clients don't come down here. It's best if you dress like Itsumi-san. Wear something comfy, something roomy." While Goto spoke, Itsumi did a little twirl for me. Is this what Goto had meant by *like home*? Under her apron, Itsumi was wearing a polo shirt and black cotton pants. "Feel free to wear sneakers. Jeans are okay, too, as long as they don't have holes in them. But no shorts or tank tops."

On the day of the interview, I used the stairs on the north side of the building, but the shredder station was on the south. My first day at the job, I looked for a door on the south that led to the basement, but couldn't find one. I wound up going around to the same door as before, on the north side, and headed downstairs from there. Walking in, I gave my best hello to the overweight woman at the reception desk. She looked shocked, but managed to say hello back, just above a whisper, before looking down again. Maybe coworkers don't say hello here? Maybe she doesn't know I work here? Maybe permanent employees don't really interact with the rest of us? I'd never been fond of salutations anyway, so I made up my mind to limit my hellos to Itsumi and Goto. When I got to the shredder station, someone was there, but it wasn't Itsumi. It was a man, a weirdly tall man, maybe six foot six, if not taller. His face was long and the stack of paper he was carrying looked tiny in his hands. It was 8:40 a.m., and no one was there except for the tall man and me. I didn't know how many of us there were in the department, but there had to be more than two. Across the way, the Print Services islands were more or less full. The workers sat in their chairs, staring at their screens. At the printing station, there were maybe fourteen people in jumpsuits and aprons, talking in small groups or starting on their work. Just then, a heavy, older guy dragging one foot came over to the shredder station, glanced at me, and nodded. He had a thick neck and eyes that looked like tiny black beads. Itsumi arrived at 8:50 a.m., her badge showing over a dark pink hoodie. She's so tiny that I bet a lot of her clothes are actually for kids. As she walked past everyone, she quietly said hello, and they all said it back, just as faintly. Maybe she's permanent. I still had no idea who was and who wasn't. Of course I didn't. The people around the islands were all in suits, but everyone at the printing station was wearing a jumpsuit or apron. At the shredder station, everyone had an apron on, except me. I felt like I didn't belong. I didn't even know where to sit. Itsumi was supposed to have my apron for me.

"Good morning," I said, looking at Itsumi. Her mouth stretched into a smile as she beckoned me over. "Hey, let's go get your apron." I followed Itsumi through the south door, where there was a staircase, just like on the north side, and a row of tall lockers. "Just so you know, these lockers don't actually lock, so don't leave your bag or valuables back here. Keep them with you. If you have a jacket or a change of clothes, you can hang them here. Also, sometimes we have three people per locker, so don't hog the hangers. Except, well, it's not usually very crowded. Most days you can do whatever you want. You can put an extra pair of shoes in here, too, if you want. If there's no room, just leave them on top of the locker. By the way, we don't have any curtains or anything, so when you want to change you'd better use the bathroom upstairs. Anyway, this is your apron. Well, it's not *yours*. It belongs to the factory. You're borrowing it. Never take it home. We have cleaning facilities on site, too, so you don't have to worry about that. You see the number sewn in here?" Itsumi held up the apron pocket so I could see. "This is your number. Memorize it. All the aprons get sent out together and come back in a single batch. It's up to you to find yours again. Most people write the number down on a piece of paper and keep it behind their ID." My number was 13458. "Speaking of which, here's your badge. You'll need to show this to the guard whenever you come through the gate. Make sure he can see the picture." She handed me a card on a red lanyard. The card had my photo on it. At first, I had no idea where they'd gotten it. Then I realized. It was the one I'd attached to my resumé. But how'd they get it onto this card? They hadn't simply cut the photo out—this one was practically twice the size. It was maybe two inches tall. I'm so unphotogenic, I could barely recognize myself. My cheeks were puffy as always. My lipstick was a disaster. You could tell right away that I don't get a lot of practice. And I'm supposed to wear this? Every day? Of course Itsumi had a picture on her badge, too. I guess she was one of those people whose photos look just like them. "Make sure you have this around your neck at all times." Her strap was dark blue. "Tighten the strap, though, or tuck it into your apron so it doesn't get sucked into the shredder," she said, pulling an apron out of a locker and putting it on. I put mine on, too. The front was smooth. It felt industrial, like it was made of rubber or nylon. I could feel the stitching on the inside. It smelled like the cleaners. As Itsumi moved toward the shredders, music started playing overhead. "Not everyone starts work at nine, but most of us do. The bell rings at 8:55, then again at nine sharp. We have the same bell when lunch starts, at noon, and then at 12:55 and 1:00. It rings one last time, too, when the day is over—at 5:30 on the dot." Itsumi called it a bell, but it was actually an electronic melody, like the ones that play in stations when a train arrives. Opening the door, I could see the people at the islands in the distance standing at attention. Everyone from the printing station was gathered around the islands, too. Itsumi whispered, "When the first bell rings, they start their morning meeting. See how Gotchy is talking? That's because he's the head honcho here.

Well, he's the head of the Print Services Branch Office, haha."
The people at the shredder station weren't taking part in the
meeting. They lumbered toward the machines, carrying documents to be shredded. "We've got extraterritoriality. No meet-
ings for us. This is the Captain's domain. I hope he comes back
soon, though." Goto stopped speaking. Everyone applauded,
then bowed. The meeting was over. In the end, there were five
people working the shredders. "Let me walk you through this,"
Itsumi said. I thought she was going to introduce me to the rest
of the team, but she never did. I guess there's no need for contract workers to know each other's names.

"Ushiyama-san, how's everything so far?" Goto came to ask
not long after lunch, wearing a suit that was clearly too large
for him. Maybe he'd shrunk? It didn't occur to me during the
interview, but he looked a little grungy, considering his position.
Itsumi had already explained my job to me, so I hadn't had any
real problems. The work itself couldn't be simpler. The paper
goes into the shredder. When your bag fills up, you throw it
out. The documents we're supposed to shred arrive in containers,
delivered through the south door. A man carts in twelve containers of documents twice a day. "There's an elevator on the other
side of the stairs, but it's only used for loading and unloading.
transport—the men who deliver things around the factory—
typically show up around 10 a.m. and 3 p.m." They wear jackets
with TRAN written on the back. When they bring the new containers, they take the full bags with them. The first TRAN I saw
was an old man, small and muscular, running around covered
in sweat. "Right, there's something I forgot to tell you earlier,"
Goto said, almost whispering. God, what? "I imagine you know
by now what kind of work you're going to be doing here. Well,
it's best if you're careful with what you say to people outside
the factory. If people find out what you do, there's a chance you
could get contacted by people who want the documents you're

destroying." Oh. "I'm sure you know this already, but the removal of any documents from factory grounds, or any leaks of information, would have very serious consequences. You'd have to quit, of course, but the factory could also seek damages. We need to have you sign a pledge and stamp a few other documents, basically saying that you recognize this. Could you come see me around 5 p.m.? We'll need to take care of things before you leave for the day. You have your seal on you, right?" Of course I did, not that he'd asked me to bring it. I'd been through this a few times before, so I was used to the routine. But that didn't change the fact that Goto was apparently totally useless.

The closest bathroom was on the ground floor. During lunch, I went up the stairs on the south side. That floor was home to another division, completely unrelated to the Print Services Branch Office. I didn't see anyone in jumpsuits or aprons. In the bathroom, two women in pink office uniforms were brushing their teeth. They looked at me in my gray rubber apron and nodded in apparent confusion. I headed for one of the stalls and listened to them talking about some barbecue, unable to tell the voices apart. The bathroom was clean and bright. The basement had plenty of fluorescent lights and air purifiers, so it wasn't exactly dark or stuffy down there. Still, as soon as I came upstairs, I felt like I could suddenly smell the outside air. In the bathroom, sunlight shone through the frosted glass windows. When I left, I saw the exit. So there was a way out on the south side. But looking out the window, all I could see was a parking lot with a few company vehicles. At the edge of the lot was a utility hose and a plastic tub. Not exactly a cheery place. I decided I'd keep using the door on the north side. It was better that way. Beyond the lot, I could see a few unassuming buildings—one, two, or three stories high, with lush green walls. At first, the factory had looked completely gray, but once I stopped to really look at it, I saw trees, flowers, vines, and all this grass. In the past, I'd had some jobs that I could never quite figure out how to do properly, no matter how hard I tried. Maybe it's not such a bad thing to have a job that you can master on the first day. I guess it depends on how you look at it. Feeding paper into a shredder can be peaceful, as long as your machine doesn't jam or overheat. And even then, all you have to do is switch it off and move over to the next one. Itsumi told me there were always more shredders than employees. "It depends on the day, but there are usually five to ten of us working at the same time. Most work half days or only come once or twice a week. Only four of us are here for the full day. Me, the Captain, and two others, but the Captain's not here right now, so ..." I wouldn't formally meet the other two, Hanzake and the Giant, until the Captain returned.

"It's time for a commercial. Let's go drink." A week after I started working at the shredder station, the Captain came back. I figured he'd be an older man, but it was still a surprise to see him: he was wrinkly and so frail that it looked as though he might crumble any moment. It's not like his face was swollen or gaunt or anything. Maybe he wasn't that sick. "While you were gone, we added a new member to the team. We talked about it before you went to the hospital, remember? We went ahead and made a decision." "Yes, I heard. A young woman, right?" "She's already started. Ushiyama-san. Hey, Ushiyama-san, our team captain is back from the hospital. Let me introduce you." "I'm Samukawa. It's a pleasure to meet you," he said. "I'm Yoshiko Ushiyama. It's very nice to meet you." "Samukawa-san, Ushiyama-san has been an excellent worker," Goto said, tapping me on the shoulder. *Excellent?* As if he knows the first thing about me. I gave the Captain a smile. He seemed like a good person, nothing like Goto. "So, from now on, Samukawa-san will be in charge of your schedule ..." Goto said, then walked back to his seat.

"Captain! Welcome back. You look amazing." Itsumi put her shredder on pause and bounced toward us. Lunch was over, and it was going to be a while before TRAN would show up again. But if we didn't take care of the morning batch before they came, we wouldn't have anywhere to put the next set. "I appreciate it, Itsumi-san. You know, I feel recharged. Ten years younger, maybe more." "Yeah, I can see it. Ushiyama-san's been with us a full week now. She's still young, but weirdly serious for her age." "Well, it's nice to have more young women around. Itsumi-san, you must have felt a little lonely being the only gal on the team." "Captain! Ushiyama-san, don't listen to him ..." It was the first time since I'd started working here that I'd seen anyone in the shredder station actually conversing. Whenever I had questions, Itsumi was always friendly, but we'd never had a real conversation, not like this. They're always talking at the printing station. Why should things be any different for us? Maybe our team simply doesn't have anything to talk about. "Has anyone been using the Power Tower?" the Captain asked, looking at the far end of our workstation. "No! You know you're the only one who knows how to use that thing." Now Itsumi was looking, too. A piece of exercise equipment had appeared there, out of nowhere. Maybe I'd just never seen it before? A piece of clothing was draped over one of the bars. "So I did leave my jacket here. I thought I lost it somewhere," the Captain said as he went to claim his jacket, but grabbed hold of the Power Tower while he was over there. "Ushiyama-san, feel free to use this. You better be careful, though. I fell once and got scolded for it." "No one wants to use it, Captain. Unlike you, we still have our youth! Right, Ushiyama?" The Captain came down from the machine and said hello to everyone else around the station. Everyone smiled sheepishly as they shook hands with him. Even the people I'd never heard speak over the last week were now laughing at his jokes. When he was done making the rounds, the Captain turned back to Itsumi and asked, "Made any commercials lately?" Commercials? Itsumi shook her head. "What, without you?" she said, whipping her ponytail one more time and turning to the short man with the thick neck, who broke into a smile and stroked his chin. "We'd never dream of it. Without you, what's the point?" The Captain shook the man's hand one more time, saying, "Come on. We've got someone new on the team. It's time for a commercial. Let's go drink." Whipping her ponytail one more time, Itsumi now looked at the tall guy, who melted into a wordless grin. "Okay, let's make it happen. What'll it be, Captain? Moo-moo as usual? You in, Ushiyama-san? You like meat?" I didn't know what *commercial* was supposed to mean, but I liked the idea of going out for meat, so I nodded. I was sure everybody from the shredder station would go, but it was just me, the Captain, Itsumi, the tall guy, and the thick-necked man. Or—as they were introduced that evening—the Giant and Hanzake.

"That's right. Hanzake," the Captain said, turning to me. We were sitting in the yakiniku restaurant on the way to the station, waiting for our beers. "Also known as the Giant Salamander. Really big amphibian. Ever heard of it?" I glanced at Hanzake, who was wiping his face with a hot towel. He really did look like a salamander. He had a wide face and a large mouth, but his nose was small and his eyes gleamed like tiny marbles. Dabbing at his mouth with his towel, Hanzake broke into a grin. At first, I thought his way of slowly creeping around was a little weird, but once I learned what his name meant I found his movements endearing. The Captain kept going: "They're called hanzake salamanders because their mouths are so huge it almost looks like their faces are split in half." And he's okay with being called that? "Our Hanzake, you know, is amphibian royalty. The Prince of Salamanders," said the Captain, poking Hanzake in the cheek. Hanzake giggled, then spoke to me. It was the first time we'd exchanged words. "When I was little, there was a nearby river that was full of them. Salamanders. One time, my dad told me that the King of Salamanders came to him with his only son and handed him over. Meaning me. I know it was a joke, but sometimes I can't help wondering if maybe he was telling the truth. What if I really am a highborn salamander, raised away from the river, in the human world?" Hanzake blinked his beady eyes. "I mean, I don't look anything like my folks, but people have always told me I look a lot like a giant salamander. Really, I wouldn't mind, though, if it were true. Being human comes with too many problems. Legs, for instance." Hanzake kicked out his left leg and stroked his knee. "I'm pretty sure this thing wouldn't give me any problems if I were scuttling along the river bottom." Itsumi leaned toward me and said, "Hanzake-san used to work the assembly line, but a huge jack ripped into his leg. For a while, he couldn't even walk." I stared at his leg. I'd seen him hobbling around, but I'd assumed it was rheumatism or something. "When was it? It had to be the same year my son Akio was born, so it's been ten years now. There I was, new father, ready to give my all, then everything went black. I'm just glad I can work like this now, all thanks to the factory." "Because of workman's comp, right?" "Here you are," the waiter came over, unloading our beers on the table. Now that we had our drinks, everyone grabbed a paper bib and put it on. The bibs said MOO-MOO YAKINIKU and had a cartoon cow on them. The cow was wearing a bib of its own and holding a knife and a fork, its tongue hanging out of its mouth. I've always hated paper bibs, but how could I say no when the others looked so happy to put theirs on? The restaurant was maybe seventy percent full and a new group had just come in. They looked young enough to be college students. Itsumi lifted her glass and looked at all of us. The Captain straightened his back and reached for his beer. "Okay. Here's to the Captain's glorious return, and to Ushiyama-san joining the team. Cheeers!" "Cheeers!" we said after Itsumi, clinking our glasses. Before long, a big plate full of assorted meats came, with a side of kimchi. "I'm sure you know why we call this guy the Giant, don't you?" Itsumi asked as she set bits of liver, tongue, and tripe on the grill. Hm, maybe because he's freakishly tall? What I really wanted to know was, why all the offal? "Giant, how tall are you again? Six-four?" "Yep," the Giant nodded while reaching over the grill with his chopsticks, anxious to flip the liver that Itsumi had put out only seconds earlier, but she stopped him before he could. "If you touched the liver with those, don't eat with them, okay? Raw blood will make you sick," she said. "Would it, though?" the Captain asked. "With his size, I'm sure a little blood wouldn't do anything." The Giant grinned and Hanzake laughed. Itsumi and the Captain carried the conversation, while the other two sat there smiling, unless Itsumi asked them something. "Hey, Ushiyama-san, how old do I look?" Itsumi asked as she parceled out pieces of grilled tongue. "Giant, you know this already has salt on it, right?" The Giant was about to pass around the lemon that had come with the tongue, but Itsumi stopped him again. "That touched raw meat, right? Put it back. Here, give it a minute on the grill." The Giant complied. "So, how old?" Itsumi asked again, waving her hair left and right. Beautifully straight hair. When I first saw her, I was sure she was younger than me, maybe under twenty. But judging from how she talks and how she works, I had to be way off. She had a few gray hairs, too. She's got to be in her thirties, but I'd better guess low. That's what you're supposed to do, right? Just then, Hanzake and the Giant burst out laughing. "Well, well," said the Captain. "You've really outdone yourself this time. What a commercial!" He raised his glass and tapped it against Itsumi's. Hanzake and the Giant bumped shoulders and laughed even harder. "Come on, Ushy!" Ushy? "Itsumi-san's been a good big sister, hasn't she?" "Yeah, yes." "Thank you, thank you. But, Captain, I got so much older while you were away. Don't ever leave us again."

Itsumi stretched her skinny neck to finish her beer and ordered another. Hanzake and the Giant held up their empty glasses to ask for more. "Okay, the liver's good now. It's all ready. Hey, Giant, the lemon's ready." The Giant grunted and tried to pick the lemon off the grill with his weirdly long fingers, but it must have been too hot, so he picked up his chopsticks and tried again. "Lemon?" he asked me. I shook my head. "Over here, Giant. I bet lemon goes well with liver." "I bet it doesn't." I had a piece of tripe and kept working on my first beer. I never found out how old Itsumi was.

IT WAS THE DAY BEFORE THE HUNT. FLYERS HAD BEEN sent out to employees with children and posted on bulletin boards all across the factory. *Join the hunt with Doctor Moss! An event for parents and children.* In the center of the flyer was Aoyama's drawing of a family of four: a boy in a baseball cap, a girl in a sailor uniform, a father with glasses, and a mother with long hair. If I could draw, even a little, I would have gone with a grade-schooler holding a magnifying glass, on his knees, examining a thick patch of green. Or, I don't know, maybe the Forest Pantser. As a warning.

On the south side, I keep my blinds rolled up, but they're always down on the east side. I keep the windows shut, too. The cleaning facility next door is so close that the buildings almost touch. If I'm really listening, even when the windows are closed, I can hear washers and dryers spinning and irons releasing steam. Besides, even with the windows open, it's not like I'd get a good breeze. When they told me about the facility next door, I could almost see the entire east wall as a giant iron, scalding hot and hissing. It was a little noisy, of course, but it didn't really bother me once I got used to it. If anything, I liked the smell of detergent that wafted over during business hours. And it wasn't a bad place to live. In the south zone, they had a residential lot set up next to the bus depot and the waste disposal plant. In comparison, this was heaven. "Now, about your lab ..." Goto had me come to the factory two weeks prior to my start date and drove me around in a newish gray car with a factory logo on the side. "I wanted to give you a few options. You're free to choose, of course, but there's really only one location I can recommend without reservation. We looked into getting you a lab space in HQ, but honestly it'll work out best to have you live here in a two-story home where you can use one of the floors as your workspace." "Live here? At the factory?" "Uh-huh." Goto pulled out of the parking lot, headed toward the intersection, then slowed to a stop. "You never know who's watching. Be sure to obey the rules whenever you're on the premises, especially when you're driving," Goto said, turning to look in the mirror. "No one told you that you'd be living here?" "This is the first I've heard of it." "My supervisor said he mentioned it. There must have been some kind of mix-up. The speed limit here is twenty-five, so we can't go too fast. Then again, we aren't going far. It'll just be a minute." There was a sign with the speed limit on the side of the road. "Legally speaking, this is a prefectural road, you know." "It is?" "It opens up just ahead, you'll see. It runs straight through the factory, then keeps on going." "The factory really has it all, doesn't it?" "Apartment complexes, supermarkets, a bowling alley, karaoke. All kinds of entertainment, even a fishing center. We have a hotel and more restaurants than you can count. I'm not talking about employee cafeterias, either. You can have soba, steak, ramen, fried chicken, fast food. In the hotel, we've got French, Italian, sushi, teppanyaki. We have a post office and a bank, a travel agency, a couple of bookstores, an optometrist, a barber, an electronics store, a gas station ..." Goto listed places off as if he were singing a song, then he hit the brakes. A crosswalk with no signal. A man carrying a gray suit on a black wire hanger nodded at Goto as he walked across the street. Goto lifted a hand from the wheel to say hello. "We have a museum, too. Most of the work is created by factory artists and employees, but it's definitely worth a look. Of course we have our own bus and taxi companies, too." "It's like a real town." "It is. Much bigger than your average town, really. We've got mountains and forests, a giant river and the ocean. We've got our own shrine, with a priest and everything. All we're missing now is a graveyard. I guess we don't have a temple, either." "When did they decide that I'd be living here?" This place was more urban than where I was living with my parents. Their house was in the middle of what used to be a resort town, barely suburban. My university was deep in the mountains, too. This was going to be my first time living in a city. The idea of moving here didn't bother me, though. It was just happening so quickly and without my input, without my knowledge. "I was under the impression that it was written in the job description that we sent to your school. Okay, here we are." It looked like a real suburban development, full of tidy two-story homes, identically shaped and built in neat rows. Plenty of space between one house and the next, each with its own garden and two-car garage. Some of the gardens boasted gorgeous flower beds in full bloom. The road was flawlessly paved and there were dogwoods lining the sidewalks. "There are quite a few dog owners around here. We also have a vet, by the way," Goto said, backing us into a garage and putting the car in park. He got out and I did the same. All the buildings looked the same, except for the one right next to us. It was an industrial-looking one-story unit that didn't fit the rest of the block. I could hear mechanical noises coming from inside, and the smell was unlike anything in the neighborhood. In fact, it smelled kind of sweet. "This property just opened up. It's in good condition. They thought about remodeling the place, but ultimately decided there was no need. Only drawback is," Goto said looking next door, "things may get a little noisy." "What is that place?" "Cleaning facility." "Ah, I see." Well, I guess that means I won't have to do my own laundry.

"There's just one thing you need to know before we get started, okay?" The children all looked up at me as if on cue. "From here on out, we're going to be doing a lot of walking, looking for moss in all kinds of places. We're going to a place with lots of trees, really close to the forest." There actually aren't that many trees there. If you look at the spot on a map, it's not even a thousand square yards wide. But once you're inside it's unsettlingly dark. "When we get there, we're going to be doing some exploring. Now, when you're hunting on your own, absolutely no going into the forest. Got it? It's really dark in there, even in the middle of the day. It's dangerous and you could get lost. The same goes for parents, okay?" They really could get lost—more than that, though, there's a creep called the Forest Pantser who runs around the area, but I'd been instructed by Aoyama to refrain from bringing him up. "You'd just ruin the mood. Everyone already knows about the guy anyway. Really, you don't need to say anything. Just make sure nothing happens. If you'd like, we can have some of the young guys from PR stand watch around the forest. We can ask security for help, too." "Good thinking, let's call security." So I thought it'd be reasonably safe, but I still didn't feel great about it. From what I'd heard, the Forest Pantser was a middle-aged man, maybe a little on the elderly side, who ran around the forest trying to pull the pants off men and women of all ages. "Why do people call him that, though?" "That's what he calls himself, apparently." Whenever his would-be victims fought back or resisted, he retreated into the trees. Of course, everyone puts up some kind of fight, so he hadn't actually removed anyone's pants. "It's not like he exclusively targets young women or anything. He'll go after anyone. All we know is wearing a suit seems to be the best deterrent." Aoyama tugged at the collar of her ash-gray suit, twisting the gold chain around her neck. There was a black stone at the tip of her necklace, almost too small to see. "I mean, it's not like he's a real sex offender." I understand that he's equally prone to prey on old men as young women, and I get that suits apparently repel him, but that hardly means he's not a pervert. Anyone running around calling himself a Forest Pantser has to be screwed up on some level. "Shouldn't someone report this guy to the cops?" "Well, he hasn't done any real harm to anyone, and every department across the factory has already issued warnings, so at this stage there's no real reason to get law enforcement involved." I think I get why the factory is reluctant. Considering how tight security is around here, it's hard to imagine the culprit sneaking in from outside. It's extremely likely that the guy's on payroll. Either way, if word got out, it wouldn't look good—but there was no guarantee that he wouldn't lay his hands on children. We had to be vigilant. Aoyama handed me a single copy of this year's flyer. "Did you need more? Were you going to pass them out?" "No, one's fine." Who was I going to give them to? "Okay, I'll reach out to security. I'll see you the morning of the hunt." Aoyama bowed once and left the lab. She got into the company car in the parking lot, bowed once more, then drove off. I collected her cup from the coffee table and washed it out. I took another look at her flyer. It didn't feel right to have Aoyama do this kind of work, especially now that she'd been promoted to manager. But at some point, she became my point of contact and these things always fell on her. I guess I wasn't entirely unhappy about it, though. She was the only one I could really talk to. And what's not to like about working with a smart and beautiful woman?

Fifteen groups of parents and children had signed up for this year's hunt. In every group, one or both of the parents worked for the factory. Two pairs had participated the year before. After the event, a few of the children, especially the older ones, wrote reports on their experiences; a handful had even won prizes and honorable mentions in the prefecture-run Junior Scientist Contest. A number of the parents wanted to hold the hunt during the summer so that their children could write about it for their summer essays, but fall is the best season for moss. The Junior Scientist Contest had a November deadline anyway. So, with the sole exception of the first hunt, which we did in spring, the event had always taken place during the fall. When I got to the west gate, five groups had already gathered there. Most of them were pairs, one parent to each child, but one of the parents came with two children—a brother and sister. There was still a little time before the hunt began, but I asked the children who were already there to get started by looking at the roots of a plane tree. "See this here? This is moss. Believe it or not, this stuff can grow anywhere!" I pinched it so they could see. Four of the kids were squatting around me in ratty-looking clothes, looking at the moss and then looking up at me. The other two, the brother and another boy, were talking about trading cards, their spit flying everywhere, saying that they'd left their rarest cards at home, but they definitely had them. The kids had never met before, but they looked like they could've been twins. I couldn't even tell their reedy voices apart. They clearly shared a passion. They squirmed with glee as each boy tried to convince the other that his cards were more valuable. The list of items to trade was extensive, and the rivalry felt very real. To keep them from coming to blows, their mothers had to step in and attempt to settle matters amicably. The sister, who looked like she was about to enter middle school, ignored her little brother completely. She joined the other kids who were playing with a patch of silvery-green moss. I couldn't tell if they were having fun, trying to look like they were, or if they were just bored out of their minds. No matter how many years I did this, the kids never made any more sense; they were utterly incomprehensible. "It kinda feels like a kitty," the girl said as she stroked the moss. Cats and moss are nothing alike. If you want to pet a cat, go pet a cat. I put on a smile and said, "This stuff can grow anywhere. A sidewalk, the rim of a volcano, even really cold places like the South Pole. That's how tough it is." "Moss can grow on ice?" the sister asked. I was grateful for the question. "Actually, there's a lot of land in the South Pole, under the ice. Sometimes it gets so cold the moss will freeze, but moss is so strong that it can survive that. As long as the temperature reaches a certain point, and it gets some moisture, it will turn green again. I'll explain more once the rest of the group is here." Once it was time, I counted to make sure everyone had arrived. The boys who'd been talking about trading cards had obeyed their mothers and put their feud on hold. There were sixteen kids and seventeen chaperones. Only two children had both of their parents with them, but the rest had either their mother or father, except for this one kid who showed up with his grandfather instead. The boy and girl who had also participated last year brought their prizewinning reports and the samples they'd collected over the past year. "My name is Yoshio Furufue, and I'll be showing you around the factory today. It's nice to meet you all." There was moss everywhere, all around the factory. I handed every kid a miniature magnifying glass along with a folded sheet of kraft paper for keeping samples, hoping the day would turn out okay.

"Furufue-san, Furufue-san. Sensei." My live-in laboratory had an intercom, but he didn't bother using it. He must have had his mouth up to the window next to the front door, which I'd left cracked open. The voice I heard was too loud to be coming from outside. I was sitting at my computer, drafting a report on the moss hunt for Aoyama, when the voice interrupted, breaking my concentration. I looked at the window. I'd seen that face before. It was the old man who'd come to the hunt with his grandson, the kid who found the body of a dead coypu. How did he know where to find me? I didn't know if I should open the door, but our eyes had already met. I couldn't remember his name, but I could picture his grandson's face perfectly. The child had eyes like sardines and a giant forehead. He was a real somber kid. The old man was definitely the livelier one. Still, the boy did pretty well during the hunt. After a moment, I stood up to open the door. I didn't feel quite right about ignoring the old man after he'd spent the whole day moss hunting with his grandson. When I went to let the man in, the boy was standing right there next to him. I guess he was too short to see through the window. The kid was wearing a dark green shirt with red and yellow stripes. Was this supposed to be his autumn shirt? By the way, shouldn't he be in school? The old man was wearing a factory uniform, one I'd never seen before, with the logo on the chest. "Can I help you?" I asked. He lowered his head and smiled. "Sorry to drop in on you like this. We wanted to thank you for organizing the moss hunt. It was truly eye-opening. Ever since, my grandson's been collecting samples at school." This made the boy blush, but his gaze didn't falter. "I'm glad to hear it. Your grandson has a keen eye. I hope he keeps hunting." "Thank you, that's very kind of you," the old man said, reaching into his chest pocket, pulling out a small square towel, and wiping his neck, even though he wasn't sweating. I bet his sweat glands had shriveled up and died ages ago. "So what brings you here today?" I asked. He craned his neck to see inside. "I hate to bother you, but would you mind if we came in for a minute?" Out of nowhere, a thick binder appeared in the boy's hands. He had a look on his little face like he was itching to get rid of it. "Actually, I'm working right now. Can I ask what it's about?" The old man smiled and grabbed the binder from his grandson. "I apologize for just showing up like this. I asked someone for your address. I used to live around here, too, a long time ago. We took the bus over and walked the rest of the way. I looked for you in the directory, but couldn't find your number or email address." "I'm in there, but my section is password-protected. Not many people need to speak with me, and this is my private residence. So, what exactly can I do for you?" Is he going to ask me to read his grandson's essay? I wasn't thrilled about the idea of reading a binder full of this kid's scribblings, but honestly I wasn't too upset about it, either. Green-roofing—my work with moss—was slow going. Reading some kid's report was the least I could do. It's not like there was much else I could do for the factory. "Do you think you could let us in first? I'd rather not tell you out here." Just then, a small truck carrying dirty laundry pulled up next door, and the gate to the cleaning facility swung open. It was probably just my imagination, but I thought I caught a whiff of the sweet smell of detergent. A middle-aged woman in an apron called out to the driver. They burst out laughing as they loaded the containers of clothing onto a dolly and steered it inside. "Okay, come on in. The place is a mess, though." "Don't worry about that, sensei. We appreciate it."

"Look here. This is called gray moss. You see that tiny blip at the tip?" "That's a bud," the sister shot back, beaming with confidence. But flowers don't grow on moss—it was most certainly not a bud. "Good guess, but remember what I said? These fellas are flowerless plants. They don't have seeds, either." I'd had Aoyama diagram the life cycle of moss on the computer, enlarge it, and print it onto a giant board of coroplast. I'd just explained to them how mosses reproduce, but I guess that sort of thing can be hard for little kids to grasp. Hell, I bet most high school biology students struggle with the subtleties of the sporophyte stage. The younger ones nod along like they're following, but there's no way that they've comprehended even half of it. They understand what I'm saying like they understand that they can drop a holiday card in the mail and it'll show up at grandma's house a couple of days later. It's not like anyone's going to quiz them on what they've learned, so why should it matter anyway? "This is a capsule. It's full of spores. The moss sends those spores flying into the air and if they land in the right kind of place they'll grow." "Just like when you blow on a dandelion, sweetheart," one of the mothers added for her daughter's benefit. I thought about responding, but decided against it. What a day. Luckily, the Forest Pantser didn't show up, but during a break the old man's grandson wandered right up to the edge of the forest, where he found some monk's moss growing among the excrement and animal carcasses. There, on the belly of a dead coypu, he found a particularly thick clump of moss. The animal might have been six feet long, but coypus shouldn't be anywhere near that size. Maybe I was imagining things. "I hear they're breeding in the sewers under the factory. Are you safe there?" one of my old university colleagues asked in an email. "It's fine. They sleep all day, and even if you get close to one, they couldn't care less about human beings," I replied. "I'm more worried about the black birds here. They look like shags or cormorants, but I still haven't identified them. There are tons of them, living by the river. Every time I look, there's more of them, too, as if the population's doubling each year. And they're not the least bit afraid of people. You can walk right up to them and they won't fly away." Back before I'd given up on the idea of green-roofing, I was walking all over the factory, looking for moss samples that might prove useful, and headed down to the riverbank to see if I could find some moss. By the river, I saw the birds, the same birds I'd seen on the hike. "This is our river. Around here, we just call it the river, or the big river." Numerous metal ladders lead down from the bridge to the river, but they're blocked off so that only maintenance can access them. The only way to get down to the river is by crossing the bridge, then walking all the way from the other shore. I could see birds at the edge of the water, their oily bodies glistening while they stared at the factory. As I got closer, a couple of them flapped their wings, but none actually took flight. They'd hop a few yards, then land again, almost like pigeons at a train station. It didn't matter what time of

49

day, there they were. Where the river narrows, water from across the factory pours out from a system of drains. While some of that water looks milky or gray, most of it seems clean. The drains are wide enough in diameter that they're never truly full with water. Coypus occasionally pop their heads out from the holes. Sometimes hot water pours out of the drains, and the coypus sniff inquisitively at the steam. The first time I saw a living one, I froze. But it didn't run away or turn toward me. It was as if it hadn't even noticed me. "Oh, right. I got so caught up telling you about the south zone that we walked right past it. Recently, a few people have spotted coypus—basically, really large rodents—along the banks of the bridge we just crossed. Has anyone here seen one? I'm guessing not. Really? Aoyama-san?" "Not today, but I'm pretty sure I've seen one before." "Huh. So, the coypu is related to the rat. You can find them here, in the factory, and all over the country, really. I have no idea why, but apparently they were brought to Japan a long time ago. Eventually they got into the wild. I don't know where they're from originally, but wherever it was, it definitely wasn't Japan. In the factory, they've only been spotted here, near the river. From what I hear, they've been around for years, and more sightings are reported every year. I've heard that maintenance has had some issues with them in the drains. If you've seen pictures of coypus, they look pretty cute, but don't try to feed them. I don't know what they eat, but please don't leave any food outside for them." Coypus eat grass, obviously. They're not by the river for the meat, and they're too slow to prey on birds. I used to see them only around the drains, but recently I've seen a few out in the open. They must be running out of space in there. Still, how did this one make it to the edge of the forest? It's nowhere near the river. "Maybe it was looking for a new home?" "It's possible. You didn't touch it, did you?" "Uh-uh." "Why would we do that, sensei?"

"SO WHAT DID YOU BRING FOR LUNCH?" KASUMI WHIS-pered. It didn't take me long to read through the booklet, no more than an hour. Once that was over, I got started on a large-format three-page printout, a blueprint for a machine, but I had no idea what kind. There was some writing in English, probably a list of parts and instructions. In the same packet was a stapled handbook and a one-page list of terms in Japanese and English. Inside the handbook, I found the same blueprint, but with text in Japanese. I figured that I was probably supposed to use the list to make sure that the English and Japanese versions matched up. I looked at the cover of the Japanese version. At the top, it said EO-1987-POGI OPERATION MANUAL 16TH ED. Under the title was an image of a globe, but it clearly wasn't a manual for globes. I read through the whole thing, and still had no idea what kind of machine it was for. The cross section was circular, and I could tell that there was some sort of electrical wire running through it. That was all. "Lunch? Nothing." Kasumi tilted her head and asked, "Then what are you going to eat?" My girlfriend had told me the factory was full of options: cafeterias, restaurants, and convenience stores. "I figured I'd just grab something around here." "Around here?" she opened her eyes wide and smiled. "All the shops are pretty far from here. We have food trucks, but it's too late to beat the lunch rush. By eleven or so, the lines get really long. They'll sell out before you can buy anything. The closest shop is always crowded and it's a fifteen-minute walk from here. The closest cafeteria is even farther ..." So she wasn't smiling. I guess that's how she looks when she's concerned. "I'm sorry. I should have mentioned this sooner," she said, tapping her cheek. "I guess I assumed your girlfriend would have told you about that ... Now that I think about it, though, why would she know?" "No, it's my fault. Anyway, I don't mind walking. You said fifteen minutes? That'll work. I'm a quick eater. Could you tell me which way to go?" "Sure. It's easy. Go the opposite way from how you got here, and when the road comes to a fork, turn right. You'll see a bunch of people headed that way." The lunch bell rang. The women across from us bolted up. The older one bent back until her vertebrae popped. "Another slow morning, huh?" "Really? Mine was pretty rough." The older one looked at me. "We always bring something. You should do the same. It's cheaper that way. You married?" "No." "Well, just cook some rice the night before. These days there are all kinds of frozen foods, so you can just heat something up and have that with the rice. Don't even consider buying lunch here. Even the cheaper options run around 400 yen." "Thanks. I'll give it some thought. In the meantime, I should go buy something, so ..." "You'd better hurry or all the good stuff's gonna be gone." And she was right. The food trucks were sold out, and by the time I'd pushed my way through the crowds to the nearest convenience store, it was almost 12:30. By then, all I could find was two energy bars and a bottle of tea. When Kasumi saw my lunch, she gave me that same smile, then offered me a tangerine: "Take this. It has lots of vitamins." I thanked her and bit into my energy bar while staring at the blueprints I'd been working on before lunch. "Ushiyama-san. Look at that face you're making. If you don't use lunch to rest your eyes, you'll burn out before the day's over," Kasumi said as she handed me another one of those hard candies with the chocolate filling. I still had one from earlier, so now I had two. "Um, can I ask you to take a look at this list? Does this Japanese look funny to you? It doesn't look right to me." "It's fine!" Her breath was awful. "Re—really?" "You're so serious, Ushiyama-san." Kasumi's face distorted, until I found myself staring at my girlfriend, smiling through a mouthful of melting chocolate. "Oh," I said, blinking hard. Kasumi excused herself, grabbed the orange tube of toothpaste and the pink toothbrush off her desk and hurried toward the door. Once she was gone, the older woman (I could see the name IRINOI written on her ID) started to talk in a voice ruined by heavy drinking. "Okay, it's now or never. Can't let Kasumi-san keep him all to herself. Hey, care for a little treat?" She was holding a cookie shaped like a chrysanthemum. "Hey, what about me?" Glasses (I couldn't see her nametag) handed me a teardrop-shaped sweet wrapped in silver foil topped with a tiny banner. "It's Hershey's. Do you like American chocolate? I know some people can't handle it." "I think I can." It's just chocolate, right? "Thanks." "We don't get a lot of young men here. I hope you can stay a while. But you won't, will you? As soon as something else comes up, you'll be gone, right?" I wouldn't answer that even if we worked for the same agency. "Haha," I said, shrugging. "Of course you will. And that's how it should be. You gotta have backbone. You can't stay in a place like this. How'd you wind up here anyway?" "I thought Kasumi-san said that his girlfriend works for their temp agency ..." "Just because his girlfriend works for some temp agency doesn't mean he has to work for them. So, what happened? Downsizing?" I don't know why, but I guess I let my guard down. "That's right. Downsizing. I was permanent, too, but ..." It didn't seem like a good idea to discuss my plans for the future, but what harm could it do to talk about the past? "I was a systems engineer. Then they let me go, just like that." "Oh no!" Glasses squealed as she put her hand up over her mouth. "That's so saaad." "That's the way things are now, though. It's not just me," I said, looking at the clock. "Well, you really should change jobs if something else comes along. I don't know much about engineering, but I'm sure it's nothing like this." "No, you're right. This is all new to me, but now that I'm here, I may as well give it my all." Right as I said that, the bell rang and Kasumi came back. 12:55. Irinoi and Glasses both grabbed pieces of gum out of the containers on their desks and started chewing. "Okay. Four and a half hours to go." "Irinoi-san, it's a little early to start counting down," Kasumi said, quickly noticing the growing collection of goodies on my desk. "How nice. Look at all those snacks," she said, smiling. It was already 1:00, so I got back to the printout. Staring at the ink, the words started to break apart, failing to hold their meaning—all I could see was a meaningless arrangement of squiggles and dots, symbols and patterns, running on endlessly. Words are such unstable things.

One Monday morning, when I got to work, there were walls between the desks that hadn't been there when we'd left the week before. Up to that point, our desks had been arranged into stations with four seats, one set near the window and the other near the door. We'd been sitting two per station, diagonally across from our station partners, but now there were thick partitions surrounding each desk. Nonpermanent staff don't work over the weekend, so they must have hired contractors to come in and install them. I know we're just temps, but how insensitive can they be? There's no way they could have set up these barriers without rummaging through our desks and personal property. When I walked in, Irinoi was already there. I fumbled through a hello, then made my way to my usual seat by the window. I felt as though I'd entered a cubicle made to fit exactly one person. There was enough space for me to do my work, but not much else. The new walls were made of metal, covered with something like carpet so you could tack papers onto them. They were about five feet tall, so you could see over them if you were standing, but sitting at your desk all you could see was a screen of fabric. I bet Kasumi, short as she was, couldn't see over them, even on her tiptoes. What made them decide to put these walls in? They probably spent a good amount of money doing it, too. But it definitely seemed like one of those decisions that everyone involved should know about beforehand. "Wow, what—what is this?" Kasumi said as she came in, walked to her desk and put her bag down. It was hard to have a conversation without both of us standing up. I got up so I could see her. "Hey, it was like this when I came in this morning. Did you know this was going to happen?" She shook her head and took off her jacket. "No . . . I can't believe it. What's going on?" We went to sit at the same time. Maybe they thought these dividers would help with our productivity. Maybe they weren't wrong. I wouldn't get distracted when Kasumi popped a piece of candy into her mouth every ten to twelve minutes, or whenever the other women started talking or laughing. I still had no idea what the younger one was named. Irinoi was always calling her Maimi or Mamimi or something, but she wore her name tag backward so no one could read it. No more awkward grins, either, when I yawned or sneezed only to find them looking at me. This'll definitely make it easier to stay focused. That has to be why they had the dividers installed: to increase our productivity. Before the next bell, I put everything they'd moved back to where it had been, then continued comparing the documents I'd been working on the week before. Nothing out of place. I bet it was two copies of the same printout. By now, I understood that, simple as they seemed, it was the documents with no obvious mistakes that were the most demanding. When there's no reason to use your pen, it's just your eyes and head that get worn out, and you're constantly second-guessing yourself, wondering if you failed to catch some glaring error. Then, I look again and inevitably find something, usually some huge mistake. It always makes me doubt my value as a professional reader. Every time I see an ad for a correspondence course in proofreading, I'm tempted to go for it. I feel as though I'll never develop like this, just sitting around, checking these documents. Besides, there's no reason to think anyone even sees the documents once I've checked them. All I know is that the completed jobs are collected and taken somewhere, but I have no idea where they go or who receives them. I have no clue if I'm doing my job correctly, so how could I hope to get better? It's pretty obvious that asking Kasumi or the others for help would be totally pointless. I'm going to have to figure this out on my own. As soon as the first bell rang, I started flipping through the papers on my desk. Same as always, Maimi or Mamimi or whatever her name was barely made it into the office in time. She looked at her desk, now cut off from the rest of the world, pulled the candy-shaped earbuds out of her ears and said, "Wait, what? Where'd the walls come from? What's the big idea?" You're a temp. Try showing up a little earlier. She took off her girlish knit cap and started talking to Irinoi: "Hey, listen to this, Irinoi-san. He failed again!" "Your brother?" "Yeah, the stylist test or whatever. I swear, he's such an idiot. And my mom—my mom bought another DVD box set, some Korean drama." The bell rang again. It was 9 a.m. They lowered their voices a little, but just kept on chatting. Dividers clearly meant nothing to them.

> Dear Customer: We have betrayed the trust that you and the people of this nation have placed in us over the years, and we wish to beg your forgiveness. All products with serial numbers ending between B44 and B67H and manufactured in 2007 or 2008 are subject to a mandatory recall. We apologize for any inconvenience. We kindly ask that you contact your nearest dealer or distributor as soon as possible. Please

be careful when handling tablets with white backs and orange, blue, or pink fronts. Note that products may change color upon exposure to humidity. Your product will be inspected or repaired, free of charge. We will assume responsibility for any costs related to inspection or repair. Should a replacement be necessary, the manufacturer will provide you with an approved item of comparable value. If you are experiencing any additional issues (smoke, noise, change in flavor, stickyness, etc.) with our other products, don't hesitate to contract your closest dealer or distributor. Your item will be inspected, even if it is not covered under the current product recall. Please except our sincerest apologies. Every member of our community, including new president, sees this as an opportunity for introspection and inprovement. We beg your forgiveness and pray for your continued how have you been? On the right, constitutional issues to the north Japanese imperial powers among the production and consumption of developed nations uses of filesharing softwhere in the pastperfect access permanganicacid in brackets when the Kyoto Protocol took effect in 2005 no, no one else. When my brother finishes cosmetolog011111001 in the south were many black ...

ITSUMI AND THE CAPTAIN SWITCHED TO SHOCHU. I OR-
dered a lemon sour. It had been a long time since I'd been out
drinking, and it didn't take me long to get buzzed. Dipped in
tare sauce, the tripe was really good, but right after I swallowed
it, I thought I could feel it coming up again, so I started talking
a lot, hoping that would help keep everything down. I started
talking about my past, my struggles. It was my own voice, but
it didn't sound anything like me. I didn't even know if it was my
turn to talk, but I kept going. Chopsticks in hand, Itsumi tended
to the grill, now and then saying, "This one's ready." "I'll take
it." I'm always taking shit from everyone. At least I used to, up
until now. "I could go for another dish of kimchi." "I think I'm
ready for noodles." "I want the bibimbap, but not the stone-
roasted one, the other one." "Kim, kimchi, noodles." "I'm ready
for another drink—so I'll go with kimchi and, yeah, maybe I'll
get the noodles." "What about you, Ushiyama-san?" I decided
to get noodles, too, and another lemon sour. "Hello, we're ready
to order." The waiter Itsumi flagged down informed us that the
noodles would take some time, so we went with liver sashimi,
kimchi, and more drinks instead. As soon as the order was in,
Itsumi turned back to me and asked, "Ushiyama-san, what do
you think of the job?" Itsumi and the Captain can really handle
their liquor. "You don't change much when you drink, either,

Ushiyama-san." But that's not true. I get really hot. I burn up. More than that, I talk a lot more than I should. Itsumi's mouth curved into a smile, but behind her glasses her pupils appeared shrunken and lackluster. I tried to talk, but the inside of my mouth was sticky. I plucked an ice cube from my glass and put it in my mouth, then spat it back out. The cold hurt. What do I think of my job? It was easy enough. I didn't think I'd made any disastrous errors so far—and I didn't see myself making any in the future. Everyone was nice, too. They were kind. I didn't need to use my head. But there was something almost vicious behind Itsumi's question. What did she want me to say? Just then, the liver came. I grabbed a piece off the plate and threw it in my mouth. It was still frozen.

"What kind of work are you doing there?" my brother's girl-friend asked. Goto warned me about saying too much to out-siders, but I hadn't come across any document that was worth leaking, that I could possibly be paid for. Any secret worth protecting wasn't going to end up at the shredder station. De-partments would handle anything that sensitive internally. It's obvious if you think about it. So why not tell her? When I said I work in print support, shredding documents, she jerked back and said, "Seriously? You mean you're on your feet all day?" Well, I have a chair. I'm sitting most of the time. Of course our chairs are old hand-me-downs from who knows what department. The cloth of my seat is in tatters, with a disintegrating layer of jaundiced foam underneath. It's on rickety casters, and there's a knob under the seat so you can adjust the height, but as soon as you put any weight on it, the seat slips back down to the lowest setting. When I'm sitting, I can't feed the machine comfortably. My hands get tired, but standing all day is out of the question.

When I get to work in the morning, I walk downstairs, open the basement door, pass the Print Services Branch Office, and head to the lockers. As I make my way across the floor, Goto and the others are seated, looking at their computers, dusting the printers or chatting among themselves. At the shredder station, Hanzake's there, and ever since we went out for yakiniku with the Captain, he's said hello in the morning. "Morning." "Good morning." I pass through the shredder station, open the door on the other side, and go over to the lockers, where I take off my jacket—if I'm wearing one—grab my apron, and put it on. I tuck my badge inside my shirt, to make sure it doesn't get chewed up by my shredder, and tie the apron straps tight around my waist. Then, back at the shredder station, I sit down at my usual chair, in front of my usual machine. Before TRAN brings the morning load, we still have the leftover paper from the day before, so there's work to do as soon as we arrive, but honestly there's no rush. To begin with, the others don't even show up early. I feel terrible if I'm not there by 8:30, but that's just my personality. When I show up, Hanzake's usually the only one there. Most mornings, I'm second to show, but sometimes the Giant's there before me. Either way, once I'm seated and ready to go, I'll pull out the book I brought with me and start reading. Meanwhile, Print Services is getting livelier by the minute. They're unpacking paper, talking about the night before, sharing sugary snacks. As a rule, the people sitting in chairs at the islands are quiet, but everyone joins the conversation when something like golf comes up. Itsumi never shows before 8:50 a.m., and most of the time she arrives after the first bell. Once a week, the Captain doesn't come in until the afternoon: "Well well well. Look who's too good to start in the morning." "You know I can't keep the nurses at the hospital waiting." "A real ladies' man, that's what you are." When the first bell sounds, Print Services starts their morning meeting and I close my book and get to it. The mouth of the shredder is the same size as the length of B4 paper. We have one shredder that can handle A0 size, but we almost never use it. When I first saw that gigantic machine,

I had no idea what it was. It looked more like a kayak than a shredder. I only figured it out when somebody from Print Services came over with a giant roll of paper and fed it to the machine. Things like that happened from time to time: someone from Print Services would waltz into our territory and use our machinery—but they have a regular-size shredder in their own area, so it doesn't happen very often. Flipping on the main power to the shredders, I pull paper from yesterday's load and set up a ten-gallon trash bag. The bags fill twice in the morning and three times in the afternoon. We mostly shred standard A4-size documents and feed them in lengthwise. For a seamless feed, you grab the next stack with your left hand while loading the paper with your right. The machine tugs on the paper, drawing your hand toward it, almost like a handshake. At first, I couldn't keep myself from giggling. Once the shredder starts sucking the paper in, you pull lightly so there's no slack. You do this to keep the paper from crumpling as it passes through the blades—otherwise the machine jams, crunching to a halt. Too many sheets at once guarantees a jam, so the ideal method is a steady stream of fewer sheets. Using one shredder for too long will make it overheat, and when that happens you move on to the next machine. We have more shredders than employees, so we can switch from one machine to another with ease. The first time I did, it almost felt like I was choosing my own partner, like I was an active member of society. Of course, that feeling didn't last. From my second day on the job, barring the occasional jam, I never had to use a single brain cell.

My brother said he was going to bring his girlfriend home. I was hoping he'd do it when I was at work, but since all three of us had the same days off, there didn't seem to be any way around it. I figured I'd just go hide in the convenience store while she was visiting, but she showed up half a day early. The three of us ended up having tea together, then we went to the tonkatsu place near our house to eat. She arrived carrying five chocolate croissants. Considering the size of her face, all of her features seemed slightly too small. Only her mouth looked large, spanning her face, revealing deep wrinkles every time she spoke or smiled. I bet some people find that likeable. She's using liquid lipstick to cover up the wrinkles around her mouth. Orange beige—a shade natural enough that most men probably don't realize. Dark brown eyeliner to make her eyes stand out. Fake eyelashes, too, the kind that almost look natural. She was tall and thin. I guess she wasn't completely revolting. Her long black hair was almost exotic. In a way, she looked more Asian than Japanese. My brother gave me a look like he knew what I was thinking. His girlfriend had a permanent position at a major temp agency, where she worked as a sales rep and coordinator, connecting temp workers and businesses. "We have a lot of people at the factory. You wouldn't know it by looking, but I think more than half the employees there are nonpermanent. It's the same for all the big corporations these days." Then she looked at my brother and asked, "She's a temp, right?" I'm right here. "Contract worker," he said, drinking his tea. "It's been forever since I've had tonkatsu. I'm going to order the pickled plum and shiso cutlet with fried shrimp set. What about you, Yoshiko?" Me? "I'll have the special pork loin," my brother said. I got the fillet cutlet. For whatever reason, my brother's girlfriend started talking about the types of women who do temp work. "So there are two types. One type—you're just like why are you even doing this? Know what I mean? They're super-talented, bright women. Then there's the total opposite. You need to teach these girls everything, literally. How to say good morning, everything." "It sounds like most of them are just hopeless," my brother said, drinking more tea. I could hear oil sizzling in the kitchen. The restaurant was maybe half full, and most of the customers were families. "It's actually split right down the middle. But that still means half of them have no real value. But my agency has to try to present them to companies as valuable, right?" My food arrived first. "Don't wait for us." I snapped my chopsticks and got started. As soon as I did, my brother's special loin came, but his girlfriend's cutlet and shrimp set was nowhere to be seen. She kept talking, tracing the rim of her teacup with one finger. "Every company uses temps to cut costs, but things never go the way they want because they're not investing in their own talent. And when things go badly, they just bring in new people, but that never works out. Well, I guess I'm the last person who should admit this, but still ... It goes the other way, too. If the temp doesn't like it, she'll just quit. She's thinking she shouldn't have to work so hard, blah blah blah. But it makes you wonder. Is that how you're going to do things for the rest of your life? I mean, it's fine when you're still young. Things'll work out. But when your parents get older or you have your own family to look after, you kinda need to do things right. There's nothing wrong with temp work, though. If you can make up your mind, like, I'm going to do this, and give it your all, that attitude opens all kinds of doors." My brother ripped through his pork, barely bothering to chew. He called the waiter over for another helping of rice, then asked, "You really think so?" She turned to him, opening her wide mouth, showing all her teeth. "The important thing is that you give it everything you've got." "Sorry for the wait. I have the ladies' special." Her plum and shiso cutlet came with a little saucer of ponzu with grated radish in it. She picked up her chopsticks, scraped the tartar sauce from the shrimp onto her plate and asked me, "Which department do you work for again?" Print Services. It was too much work to say anything about the Branch Office. In all honesty, I wasn't even sure there was a main office. "So you make brochures? Product manuals?" In our office, we don't work on things like that. We only print internal documents, nothing that really matters. The stakes are pretty low. But recently everyone's been getting worked up over the notices about animals running wild around the factory: stray dogs and cats, crows and coypus. ("What's a coypu?" "Oh, I saw one of those." "Crazy, I mean, scary." "Not really. I wasn't scared. They're kind of like really big marmots." "You don't think a really big marmot is scary?" "They weren't here before, right?" "I don't know. I remember hearing rumors when I started. I thought they were just otters or something.") When I mentioned coypus, my brother sat up. "Yeah, I saw that on the news. They're running rampant all over the place. It's a serious problem." His girlfriend took the tartar sauce and slathered it over her cabbage. She still hadn't taken a bite, but my brother was eighty percent done. I was sure he was about to ask for more cabbage. Maybe she can't read him, but I can. Without a word, my brother grabbed my purple pickles because he knows I can't stand them. He took one big bite, then said, "They're rodents. They were imported to Japan before the war for their fur. Then they went feral. They're all over the country now. Hey, excuse me—can I get some more cabbage? Not that much." "They said that on the news. Hey, Yoshiko-chan, have you ever seen one?" Now she's calling me Yoshiko-*chan*? I felt like an iguana was crawling around my insides. It's one thing if an aunt calls me that, but it was my first time meeting this woman. What the hell was she trying to do? Maybe she thought she was being friendly, but I didn't need her friendship. I didn't want it. Every word that came out of her mouth made it that much harder to tolerate her. My brother knows how much I hate being called that, but he didn't say anything. He just kept eating. Maybe he was too embarrassed. I tried to let it go, but then she started dipping her pork in the ponzu. She took a bite, added more sauce and took another bite, even though it already had an umeboshi inside. "I think I like it better with bulldog sauce." What was my brother thinking getting involved with this hideous freak? "But, yeah, it's basically a really big rat." "Good morning." "Morning." It was raining, but the basement was the same as ever. Always the same temperature, the same humidity. A muffled, manmade air. The smell of rain clung to my clothes and hair, but that never lasted. "It's really pouring, huh?" "I know, it's horrible." At Print Services, they were talking at length about the relationship between humidity and paper quality. Maybe they have a sensitivity for the dampness of paper that we simply lack in the Shredder Squad. Rain or sleet, nothing changes for us. Same for TRAN, sweating in their jackets all year round. Itsumi rushed in, her hair all over the place, clearly upset about something. "It's too soon . . . She's only twenty years old, my daughter, my baby girl. And now she's going to have a baby of her own. What about college? What about me? I'm gonna be a grandmother." Grandmother? Out of the corner of my eye, I thought I saw one of the smaller women in Print Services holding a black bird by its wings, but when I looked again it was just a toner cartridge. The woman was down on one knee, swapping it out. She put the old one in the empty box, then TRAN came and took it away.

THE FOREST PANTSER DRESSES THE PART. UNDER A MAN-
tle of coypu fur, he wears a gray jumpsuit, an old design that no
one wears anymore. His uniform is on the baggy side, a little too
large for him. He tucks his pants into his black rubber boots. Age
has made a smaller man of him.

"Like I said last time, the first thing you should do is walk
around the factory to see what kind of moss you can find. It's
really not my area of expertise, so I can't help you any more than
that." No one could. The hike came to an end, and so did the first
moss hunt. Following that, though, there was a nebulous stretch
of nothing but time, but I suppose that was the same at the lab
at my university. Spring, summer, fall, winter. A never-ending
cycle of seasons. Back then, everything was easy for me—it was
a time of happiness. At the factory, I wake up, eat breakfast, walk
around, maybe ride around on the bus, grab lunch at the usual
cafeteria, take another walk, go back home to work on samples
or plug data into my computer. Then I eat dinner, take a bath, go
to sleep, and get ready to start the whole thing over again. How
long can this go on? My live-in lab next to the cleaning facility
has a kitchen and a bath. The cafeteria is a five-minute walk. It's
close enough to the residential areas that once in a while you'll
see married couples or families there. "This cafeteria is a little
ways from HQ, and not many of you work in the area, I'm sure,

but it doesn't hurt to know it's here. The lunch special is highly recommended. Personally, I enjoy the, uh, croquette ... What is it? Koban croquette? Aoyama-san, do you remember?" "Waraji." "Waraji croquette?" "The waraji croquette lunch special. With ground beef inside. It's sweet and spicy. You'll love it!" "It's the PR Department's favorite. We'll ride the bus over just to eat here." It's not ground beef, though. It's pulled beef cooked in sweet sauce. They serve breakfast between 7:30 and 9:30 a.m., and if you sign up for the breakfast plan, you can eat something a little different every morning—grilled fish with rice and miso, an omelet with a side of toast—all for just 5,000 yen a month. They're closed on weekends and holidays, whenever the factory is closed, so that makes it about 250 yen per day. It's a cheap alternative to going grocery shopping, getting up early, and fixing your own breakfast. Most days, I'm there for lunch and dinner, too. Still, when I'm out searching for moss around the factory, I'll make a point of trying out the local cafeterias and restaurants. Some places are awful, with rice like glue or watery ramen. But the factory has a handful of places that are amazing—if this were a real town they'd be legendary, with lines running around the corner. We've got a great dim sum stand, a French creperie, a vegetable tanmen place, and a really good BBQ spot for dining alone. We've even got an eel restaurant that delivers anywhere. I've eaten broiled eel on rice in the middle of the forest. My diet at the factory was definitely a step up from my student days, when my culinary life was pretty much limited to the school cafeteria and chain izakayas. But I didn't come here to get fat on the food. I'm not walking around the factory to burn calories, either. So why *did* I come here?

"Thank you for calling Public Relations. This is Irinoi." Huh? Illinois? "Uh, yes, this is Furufue of the EI Division Office for Green-Roof Research." "Always a pleasure." "Oh, the pleasure's all mine. Could I please speak to Goto-san?" "Sorry, could I get that name again?" "Me? Furufue." "Sorry, the name of your office, please . . ." "The EI Division Office for Green-Roof Research." "The EI Department of Green-Roof Research. My apologies, Professor. For Goto, right? One moment, please." On hold, a MIDI version of the factory anthem played. When I first heard the lyrics at the welcome ceremony, I shuddered at the loftiness of the factory's ideals, but this was just the melody. No lyrics. I'm only forced to listen to this song when I'm on hold. I can't even remember the words anymore. After two or three minutes, Goto picked up. "Sorry to keep you waiting. This is Goto. The woman who took your call wasn't making any sense." Goto was practically shouting. Could Irinoi hear him? Maybe their office was just really loud? "It's no problem. She was very helpful, actually. Is it a bad time? Do you have a moment to talk?" "Yes, yes, go ahead." "It's about greening the rooftops. Things really aren't progressing at all. I believe there's someone at HQ who okayed the green-roofing project. I hate to impose, but I was wondering if I could have a minute of their time, to discuss matters." "Discuss matters? Specifically, what were you hoping to discuss?" "Well, like I said, my work isn't exactly proceeding according to plan. I'd like to talk with HQ about the best path forward. Otherwise, I can't be sure what my next step ought to be." "It's fine. Just keep going at your own pace. We understand that it could take months, years. Don't worry about that." "That's the thing. I genuinely have no idea how long it's going to take. As things are, the factory's roofs and walls may be bare for the foreseeable future." I could hear Goto pause and take a swig of something. Something metallic clanked against the receiver. Probably a can of coffee. They say you'll get diabetes if you drink too much of that stuff. "Don't be so hard on yourself. This isn't the sort of thing you can finish overnight." "I understand that. But it doesn't feel right to continue like this. If it were a year or two, maybe. But we have no idea how much time it'll take, and I'm doing it alone." "I know what you mean. But trust me, you're doing plenty. New products always take entire teams years to develop. It's completely normal. A result-oriented approach simply doesn't make sense in Japan. Just take it easy, keep classifying your moss. The factory is a big place, bigger than you know. There are so many places we couldn't show you during the hike. At the moss hunt, you said that moss can grow anywhere. Aoyama told me. It'll take you a long time to make your way around the factory looking for moss, and there's no reason to believe you won't find new kinds of moss in the same place if you go back a month later or a year later, right? What if you made a moss map? I bet even that would take a whole lifetime to complete—a map of the moss across the factory. Just put the green-roof business on the back burner for now, okay?" I had no idea what Goto was trying to tell me. Back burner? Moss map? Sure, I mentioned a map like that to the kids during the moss hunt. "Why don't you try it? I bet it'd be fun to make a moss map of everything you find in your garden. Or all the moss you see on the way to school. When you find something, take a little sample of it, a specimen, and ask your teacher at school to help you figure out what you found! I'd be happy to help out in any way I can, too." If green-roofing doesn't matter, then what am I doing here? "You're really passionate about this, I can see that. Truly, there's no need to rush. Just take your time, try to relax a little. Let's grab a drink sometime soon," he said. I thought I could hear him reaching for his can of coffee. Clearly he wanted to get off the phone. "Well, thanks for your time," was all I managed to say. Before I could even finish, Goto said, "Okay, talk soon," and hung up.

"Here," I said, setting down a cup of black tea. "Thank you, sir. So, sensei, have you seen the black birds at the mouth of the big river?" the old man asked as he reached for his cup of tea. Black birds? "I know about the birds. There are more of them every year, completely unafraid of people. I've been to the river a few times. Sometimes, I've gotten right up next to them—they don't even flinch." I'd been thinking about these birds ever since I'd started at the factory. I actually felt kind of excited when the old man brought them up. The other employees didn't seem to pay any attention to the birds, even though their numbers really did seem to be increasing at an alarming rate. Right where the river becomes the ocean, and nowhere else, the birds roost in such great numbers you can't tell one from the next. Maybe they huddle together for warmth, or maybe there was some other reason. They almost never leave the group, there are hundreds of them, all looking toward the factory. "Sensei, do you know what kind of birds they are?" I don't. They look like cormorants or shags, but they aren't. They're not ocean cormorants or river cormorants. Their wings and bodies are black, without a hint of white or gray—jet-black birds with long necks. Usually cormorants have white faces and necks and their beaks are yellow. If I really wanted to know more about them, I'd have to take pictures and share them with an expert, but I didn't see the need to go that far. First of all, I can't lose sight of why I'm here, right? I came for the moss, not the animals. And it's not like I've even gotten a firm grasp on the moss. I don't think I ever will, either. "I'm afraid I don't. It looks like a cormorant, but ..." "That's right, sensei. It's a kind of cormorant, one found nowhere else in the world. They only live in this river, in the factory." "Only in the factory?" "Exactly. You know how, in Tokyo, there's a moat around the Imperial Palace? It's been cut off from the outside world for centuries. It's off-limits, of course, so you can't put a camera down there or throw a net in." "Right. I mean, I suppose not." "But imagine you could. Chances are good you'd find all sorts of oddities: creatures long thought to be extinct, species never before seen, animals that have followed their own unique evolutionary path. Now, keep in mind, this is happening in the middle of a metropolis, a stone's throw from the National Diet, which is to say that being cut off from the world has nothing to do with physical proximity. Similarly, the black birds in the big river belong to the factory." "But the palace has real walls, physical boundaries, which keep it separate from the world at large. That's not true here. The river runs to the ocean. They could go anywhere. All they'd have to do is fly. For that many birds to live together in a space so small would necessitate fierce competition for food. It's hard to believe that some of them wouldn't fly off to find a more forgiving environment." "But they can't fly. They can leap from spot to spot, but they never go very far." "They can't fly?" "Not the way most birds can. Which reminds me, we came here to ask you something." The old man stopped talking, took a sip of his tea, then turned to his grandson. The boy's sardine eyes were glowing, dead set on Doctor Moss. "My grandson wrote a report based on his observations of the birds. Actually, not just the birds, but a few kinds of animals that can be found around the factory. Lizards and so on. We were wondering if you wouldn't mind reading it over." The boy opened his little mouth and said just one word: "Please." I wondered if that was the first time I'd heard him speak. Did he say anything during the moss hunt? I honestly couldn't remember. "I spent a year writing it." "He started when he was in the fourth grade." When I heard that, I nodded in spite of myself, my voice only coming later: "I can take a look, I don't mind." Of course I minded. Still, I was definitely interested in the birds. I put down my tea and picked up the binder. Flipping back the light-brown construction paper cover, I could see that the report was full of college-ruled loose-leaf paper. On the first page, it said, "A Study of Factory Fauna by Hikaru Samukawa (Grade 5, Gray Valley Elementary School)." His writing was eerily tidy for a boy his age. Thinking this would be easy enough to read, I turned the page. The rest of the pages were typed out on a computer. The old man pulled a pair of silver-wire bifocals out of his shirt pocket and held them up like a lorgnette to peer at the binder with me. "He borrowed his dad's PC for this." Each printed page had been carefully cut and pasted onto a sheet of note paper. I looked at the table of contents on the first page. "Chapter One: Grayback Coypu; Chapter Two: Washer Lizard . . ." Washer Lizard? What is this? "I'm sure you already know this, but computers are very convenient. You start typing a word and it'll complete it for you." The old man put his glasses back in his pocket, let out a deep sigh, then drank the rest of his tea. "We'll leave the binder with you. Please read it when you can find time. We know it isn't really your area of expertise, but it would be great to have an actual scholar go over it. I'm always around, so once you've read it, or if you have any questions, please let me know," he said, holding out a business card and bowing. It was just a formality, to be sure, but it still took me by surprise. "Sorry, I'm out of cards right now . . . Thanks for this." I hadn't had any business cards in a few years, actually. I'm sure Aoyama would have made a new batch for me if I asked, but it's not like there's anyone I need to give my card to. I never even have the opportunity to talk to others, except maybe when I'm in the cafeteria. And it's not like I'd want to hand them out to the kids during the moss hunt. "Don't worry about that. I know how to find you. I can come and visit you here," the old man said, smiling. They left and I washed the cups. Washer Lizard? Somehow I'd let myself get caught up in some schoolboy's fantasy. I could already tell this was going to be a headache. I almost never had people over, and the strange air that the two of them had brought into my house showed no sign of clearing. I figured I might as well head out, go to the river, and look at the black birds. I decided to take my digital camera—it seemed like a good idea to get some pictures. I hadn't even taken any pictures of moss recently. When I turned the camera on, I was confronted with an image I'd taken at the wedding reception of a couple from my lab back at school. It was supposed to be their wedding cake, but I'd ruined the shot. The cake was blurry, unrecognizable. I'm pretty sure it was a chocolate cake in the shape of a violin, because the bride had played violin most of her life. Why do I even remember that? I clicked a couple of buttons and deleted the image.

ONCE I GOT USED TO THE PARTITIONS, IT ALMOST SEEMED like they were a good thing. I could take it easy, especially during lunch. I didn't have to answer any weird questions about what I was reading, or hear anyone's thoughts about which 7-Eleven bento they liked best. Better still, I didn't have to pretend like I couldn't hear the inane conversations that Irinoi and Glasses were always having. I could even take a second to rest my eyes. The only problem was that sometimes I'd fall asleep. I did everything I could to stay awake. I tracked down the mintiest gum I could find. I used mouth spray and eyedrops. I kept a cup of black coffee at my desk so I'd be ready. None of it helped. As soon as I started to feel a little sleepy, I was out cold. I wouldn't even realize it until I woke up again. And I couldn't just drink coffee or chew gum all day. I actually tried that, too, but to no avail. Some days, I'd fall asleep twice. Then I'd jerk awake. Recently, I've started telling myself that a little sleep is unavoidable—it doesn't matter how much sleep I get the night before, it doesn't matter how awake I might feel—so I might as well go along with it. A couple of times, I went to the drugstore, looking for something more serious. Some pills even worked for a day, but never longer. I bought caffeine pills, but they had no effect. I'd heard that hot food makes you sleepy, so I switched over to cold lunches, but nothing changed. Maybe it was chronic fatigue. Before I started this job,

I was always working long days, always working overtime. At this job, every day ends right on time, as soon as the bell rings. It's meaningless work that comes with no real responsibility. Maybe my body knows this and it's trying to get some much-needed rest. I bet that if Kasumi or the other temps saw me sleeping, they'd say something. So far, they hadn't said a word, which probably means they hadn't noticed. I'm giving it everything I've got, so why punish myself any more than necessary? When I pass out at my desk, when sleep takes over, I completely lose track of what I'm reading. I read the same lines over and over, hoping something will click, but it's impossible to get my head around the words on the page. At a loss, I try my hardest to keep editing—then I wake up. Honestly, half the stuff they have me read doesn't even make sense when I'm fully awake. I can't tell if the document stopped making sense because I was drifting off or if it never made sense in the first place. Corporate profiles, operating manuals, booklets for children, recipes, texts on everything from science to history ... Who wrote this stuff? For what audience? To what end? Why does it need to be proofread at all? If these are all factory documents, what the hell is the factory? What's it making? I thought I knew before, but once I started working here I realized that I had no idea. What kind of factory is this?

I grabbed an oversized packet from the stack and pulled out the contents. Inside was a paper folder. Nothing else. No additional materials, no glossaries. I guess that means I'm supposed to read it and keep an eye out for typos. I told myself I wasn't tired and flipped it open, hoping it would be something I could understand.

Chapter One: Grayback Coypu
What is the Grayback Coypu?
Classification: Rodent. A member of the Echimyidae family, similar to the spiny rat.

Size: The body measures between 15 and 30 inches. The tail can be as long as 12 inches. Most weigh about 20 pounds, but larger ones can weigh nearly 70 pounds.

Color and Shape: The grayback is covered in fur. The long fur on its back is gray and brown, but the waterproof fur on its belly is almost white. The hair on its muzzle is light gray. It has large front teeth. The grayback has a big head and tiny eyes. Its legs have short, bristly fur. Each of its four feet has five toes.

Other Features: Graybacks live near the river. They are physically well-suited to that environment, yet, compared to other coypus, graybacks are bad swimmers. While their feet are webbed, their legs are too short for them to swim for long periods of time. They use their sharp claws to rake up aquatic plants and hack away at the branches that they use to make their dens. Graybacks do not leave their dens during the day. This is because they are nocturnal. They have long whiskers and look a good deal like their close relative, the beaver. When graybacks swim, they face upward, with their whiskers above the water. Their eyes are smaller than those of other coypus, and when they swim, it looks as though their eyes are shut.

Diet of the Grayback Coypu: For the most part, graybacks eat the grass that grows in and around the river. Specifically, they feed on the leaves, stems, flowers, and roots of goldenrods, water hyacinths, and the local variety of reeds. Graybacks will also eat mice, smaller fish, and food that people throw away. They move very slowly, and cannot prey upon animals unless they are weak or dead. They cannot hunt. Because there are many places for people to eat near the river, these coypus have eaten a good deal of human food. As their diet has shifted toward discarded human food, their teeth have grown longer. Sometimes they gnaw on the concrete of the embankment and the girders of the bridge. Compared to other coypus, which eat only plants, their diet is extremely high in calories. As a result, graybacks get bigger and fatter with every year. They can reach six and a half feet in length, but a grayback this size has yet to be seen alive.

Habitat of the Grayback Coypu: Many graybacks live near the factory's river.

Originally, coypus inhabited a stretch of land from Brazil to Argentina. They were brought to Japan in the 1930s for their fur, which the military used for coats. People also cooked and ate them. After the Second World War, Japan no longer needed military clothing, therefore graybacks were no longer useful. The graybacks that remained went feral, and now inhabit river areas throughout Japan. In fact, similar cases of coypus returning to the wild have been seen around the world, in North America and Europe, for example. It seems as though the graybacks have been living in the factory for a long time. They have unique traits: a grayer body, smaller eyes, and an appetite for much more than grass. According to some, the coypus were already living in the area by the time the bridge was constructed.

There are many drains in the concrete slope along the river. The graybacks live inside them, in grass dens. The grass and branches used to make these dens often block the drains. As a result, they must be cleaned regularly. It appears that the factory is not capturing or exterminating the coypus when performing these routine cleanups. While some graybacks make their dens outside of the drains, this is uncommon. Some of the drains contain hot water, ranging from 85 to 105 degrees Fahrenheit. Interestingly, the graybacks seem to enjoy these *hot springs*. On winter mornings, graybacks may be found bathing in the steaming water, twitching their whiskers in rapture.

Life of the Grayback Coypu: Baby graybacks are born in the spring, usually in March or April, when the cherry blossoms are in bloom. In the fall, graybacks go into heat and the males approach the dens of the females. When a female allows a male to enter her den, they mate. Shortly after copulation, the male is forced out of the den. At that time, the female begins constructing a special area for childbirth in the most elevated part of her den, where water and sewage cannot reach. This special area is constructed from fine grass and stems that the female grayback has cut up with her claws. In January, roughly 130 days into gestation, the female becomes sensitive, refusing the company of other graybacks. When another coypu approaches, the female may become violent, baring her fangs and claws. After a gestation period of around 200 days, the female grayback gives birth to one or two babies, but occasionally as many as five. Newborns range in weight from 2 to 14 ounces. When they are born, graybacks are already covered in fur, but their eyes are closed. They cannot walk or swim. It takes roughly a week for the infant's eyes to open, and during this time they stay in the special den, sleeping and drinking their mother's milk. After that, they are able to open their eyes, but can still barely see. Even the adult grayback has very small eyes, but the eye of the child is no larger than the tip of a pencil. When it first opens its eyes, the baby grayback perceives only a blur of light. For up to three weeks, the young drink their mother's milk, after which time they eat the same food as adults. Younger graybacks are especially fond of human food. Graybacks reach adulthood within approximately one year of birth. Females born in the spring mate in the fall and give birth to their own children the following spring.

Graybacks leave their dens in search of food twice a day, once in the early morning and once in the evening. They travel up the river toward the factory complex or climb up the embankment. Occasionally, they head in the other direction, toward the ocean, but they never go too far, because they don't like the saltwater. When the sun is out, graybacks usually stay in their dens, sleeping. Graybacks sometimes sunbathe, just outside the drains where they make their homes. As soon as the sun goes down, they come out again and make their evening run for food. They move efficiently, and once they've found enough nourishment, they return to their dens to sleep. At nighttime, when the factory lights switch on, their eyes glow red. In one hole, a family of graybacks may live around a mother, but there is little communication among families. It almost seems as though they avoid one another out of consideration. Sometimes, multiple mothers and daughters live together in a single space, even birthing their offspring together. Yet, as mentioned earlier, pregnant females become aggressive, and when this happens younger female graybacks will be forced deeper into the drainpipe, which can be inconvenient when coming out to search for food. During mating season, conflict among female coypus is fairly common. While a male grayback may live in the same hole as a female outside of the period of pregnancy (as long as 200 days), most males will either search for a hole not currently in use by a female or make a bed of grass by the riverbank and live there. There are many drains in the area and new ones are being installed all the time. For this reason, the graybacks are never at risk of running out of inhabitable space.

The lifespan of the grayback coypu is between 10 and 40 years. As they age, the color of their fur begins to fade. They develop bald spots. On the bank, one may find clumps of coypu fur shed by elderly graybacks. In old age, their small eyes become even smaller. The aged graybacks' eyes weaken to the point that they are more or less blind, similar to newborns. As a result, they spend even more time in their dens. Most graybacks die between late winter and early spring. As they can be very large, the factory personnel who discover them may experience considerable shock. Sometimes the remains of graybacks clog the drains; for this reason, the drains are frequently inspected, particularly during this period. As a policy, the factory does not acknowledge that these inspections are carried out for the purpose of clearing deceased graybacks from the drains.

The grayback and the factory worker inhabit the same space, but rarely meet. When the grayback leaves its den during the day, it never wanders far. It may sunbathe near the mouth of the drain, out of the eye of factory personnel. Even a pregnant grayback will not attack a worker—as long as the person does not provoke it. The animal is more likely to flee. In this way, the grayback and the factory worker have managed to coexist peacefully for years.

Chapter Two: Washer Lizard
What is the Washer Lizard?

Classification: Squamata, the order of scaly reptiles.

Size: 2 to 4 inches in total length, but nearly one-quarter of this is tail. They are small lizards, weighing roughly three-quarters of an ounce as adults.

Color and Shape: The individual lizard's color varies according to the machine it inhabits, but most are gray. At birth, the washer lizard is the color of human flesh. It darkens with age. The animal is scaly and somewhat rough to the touch. Its scales have no pattern.

Other Features: The pads of the lizard's feet are covered in fine hairs, allowing it to cling to the vertical surfaces of the washing machine. When the lizard makes its nest and lays eggs, it emits a viscous liquid from its rear. This is perhaps why the washer lizard's tail is far shorter than those of other lizards. Its tongue is unusually long, and lint fibers often stick to it. Lint is central to the lizard's life. It doubles as a food source and material for its nest.

Diet of the Washer Lizard: Washer lizards prey on insects that live in the cleaning facilities. They also consume undissolved detergent and dust that is high in protein. As mentioned above, the lizard will eat lint, in addition to the bits of bread or candy left behind by the laundromat staff. They drink water that leaks from the machines, and once fully grown they will also climb on top of the machines, stick their necks into the detergent drawer and lap up the hot water. Young lizards occasionally attempt this, too, but they will likely fall into the machine and drown. This is one of the reasons that it is extremely difficult for the washer lizard to reach adulthood. I will return to this topic shortly.

Habitat of the Washer Lizard: The washer lizard can be found in both of the cleaning facilities on the factory campus. Each lizard lives alone, in a nest it makes below or behind a washing machine. The lizard may also choose to make its home in the gap between two machines. The nest generally consists of lint fibers held together by the liquid the lizard produces. Nests measure roughly four inches in diameter. Because lint is a limited resource in this environment, nests may be smaller when newly created. Most lizards prefer to find an abandoned nest and expand it over time. As a cold-blooded reptile, the washer lizard seeks out sunlight from the windows or the heat of washing machines currently in operation. It may also remain in its nest, making minimal movements throughout the day. Straying too far from one's nest may result in it being stolen by another lizard. Because of this, the lizard only rarely leaves its immediate surroundings. Throughout the year, when the facilities are closed at night and the machines are still, the washer lizard returns to its nest to sleep. In the winter, sunlight is scarce and the temperature drops significantly. This is without question the most dangerous season for the washer lizard.

Life of the Washer Lizard: The life of the washer lizard is inextricably tied to the washing machine. It never make its nest far from the machines.

The adult washer lizard lays white eggs, roughly 8 millimeters in size, during the spring or fall. They typically lay 3 to 5 eggs at once, but can lay as many as 10. The number of eggs depends on the diet of the adult and the quality of the environment. The mother washer lizard lays her eggs, then soon leaves to search for food or to claim another nest. She does not look after her eggs. The nest in which the eggs are laid is crafted specifically for that purpose. It is made of thick foam and viscous discharge. This nest is far less durable than the lint nest in which the washer lizard lives. From 9 a.m. to 5:30 p.m., the laundry units continue to run, and the nests, effectively attached to the machines, will tremble along with their motions. Because of the constant movement, some eggs may fall and crack. Depending on how long the lizard has been growing within the egg, it may hatch as a result of the fall. Washer lizard eggs are extremely fragile. For a period of time, the slime and foam keep the egg from drying out. The air in the foam also allows the unborn lizards to breathe within the egg. Yet, over time, the foam disappears and the egg dries out. After a week, the egg is practically bare. At that point, the shell dries out completely. The shell is so soft, however, that it never hardens like a bird's egg. 10 to 14 days after the eggs are laid, the young are hatched. The hatchlings climb out of the nest and move toward the washer or the wall before reaching the ground. Roughly half of the eggs laid hatch. The other eggs dry before fully developing or crack, leading to the death of the baby lizard. For this reason, the largest and strongest female washer lizards claim the most suitable spaces between the machine and wall. In these ideal spaces, there is a greater chance of successful hatching. Meanwhile, weaker females have little choice but to make their egg nests around machines that are either out of order or vibrate excessively, leaving little chance for the success of their offspring. Young lizards are smaller than adults, but similarly shaped. When they emerge from the egg, they are wet and soft. Within a day of being hatched, however, their skin dries out and becomes rougher. At first, their backs and heads are dry and rough, while their bellies and feet are relatively moist, allowing them to crawl up walls and washing machines with ease. Children and adults cling to the tops of the washers while they are in motion. It looks as though they enjoy it.

In certain cases, young lizards may mistake the dust caught in the lint trap for food and die. This will not kill adults, because their stomachs have properly developed. Hatchlings may also be eaten by the spiders that live in the cleaning facility. Additionally, adult lizards sometimes hoard food for themselves, forcing younger lizards to starve. For these and other reasons, children rarely reach adulthood. The adult washer lizard can swim—to an extent—but the child cannot. If the washing machine begins a cycle while the lizard is drinking water from the drum, it stands no chance of survival. Caught in the current, it will become entwined in the laundry. In this small space, competition is of course very fierce. Only the luckiest lizards get their fill of water, detergent, collar grime, and insects to eat. Only the select few will reach adulthood and leave offspring behind.

It takes 6 months for washer lizards to reach adulthood. Around the time they reach 3 inches in length, they begin to breed. During this period, the males appear their most reddish. The male approaches the female, with his tail high in the air, and attempts to mount her. If the female refuses, she scampers off. If she remains, they copulate. Afterward, the female lizard searches for a machine where she can lay her eggs. When she finds a good spot, she lays her eggs, then promptly returns to her former nest and continues her normal routine. The female washer lizard may lay as many as 50 eggs in her lifetime. Of course, in reality, the average figure is far lower. Not every lizard can expect this much from life.

The washer lizard has a maximum lifespan of three years. A lizard that survives this long has been extremely fortunate. Should it make it to old age, its 3-inch body may shrink. It will breathe its last without ever straying far from its birthplace, probably dying behind the machine where it nested or maybe inside the lint trap.

When the facilities are cleaned, the bodies of washer lizards are discovered in great numbers. Because the machines have not been moved out of the facilities since they were first installed, it seems reasonable to believe that there is an even greater number of lizard bodies hidden under the machines—I was unable to confirm this, however, during the course of my investigation.

Chapter Three: Factory Shag
What is the Factory Shag?

Classification: A member of the order Pelecaniformes, related to the cormorant.

Size: The body is 30 to 35 inches long, making it rather large compared to other shags.

Color and Shape: The factory shag has a long neck and a prominent crest, but its most striking characteristic is the color of its body. Its head, wings, beak, and legs are entirely black. If you were to pluck out its feathers, you would find black skin underneath. The only part of the bird that is not black is the white of its eyes.

Other Features: Factory shags have feathered wings like other birds, and can fly as far as 65 feet, typically hovering just above the river, but they do not appear to be capable of flying long distances. Shags are aquatic birds. They can swim and dive for fish. While they make their home at the mouth of the factory's river, they will not venture into the ocean.

Diet of the Factory Shag: The factory shag consumes fish and food waste. It resides where ocean water and freshwater come into contact, and has plenty of fish to choose from. The shag resembles the cormorants used for fishing. It swallows fish whole. Because of this, its tongue is very small. If you open the bird's mouth, you may not even see it. The inside of its mouth is not black, but pink. The shag eats rice, vegetable scraps, and other food that flows into the river through the factory's drains. Whatever it eats, it swallows whole. This is obvious from the shape of its neck.

Habitat of the Factory Shag: In general, cormorants and shags tend to group together in colonies. The factory shag is no different in this regard. Since this bird exclusively lives where the river meets the ocean, there is only one very large flock. The birds congregate and sleep in one spot, huddled by the shore. They dive into the water to find food, never leaving the immediate area. They appear to have no problem staying in the water all day long. When the sun is shining, the birds spread their wings and soak it in. It's almost as though they're drying their feathers out, but on days with relatively little sun the birds seem equally happy to remain wet. These birds are different from river and ocean cormorants found elsewhere. While they clearly share a number of traits and characteristics (such as living in groups or swallowing their food whole), there are several stark differences. Among these are nesting habits. While similar birds make their nests in trees (river cormorants) or on cliffs (ocean cormorants), factory shags don't seem to nest at all. They spend their whole lives in the same stretch of the river, living as one large group, never pairing off. Under no circumstances do they voluntarily leave the flock.

Life of the Factory Shag: Over the course of my observation, I have never seen any factory shag eggs or chicks. When river cormorant chicks hatch, they are featherless. Their black wings develop over time. Parents feed fish to their chicks from mouth to mouth. One might expect that these birds lay their eggs somewhere during the winter. But I have watched the flock closely, even in the winter, and have not yet found anything to suggest that this is the case. All of the birds in the flock are adults, roughly the same size. They are constantly pushing and shoving, but do not appear to communicate. In addition to finding no young, I have yet to find the carcass of a factory shag.

Where Did The Birds Come From? Where Are They Going? I have seen workers come to capture factory shags on occasion. I do not know what purpose this serves. After some time, the workers will return the birds to the ocean. Once they are tossed into the water, the shags appear to swim back to the flock or sink and die. I have not found a body, but it is very difficult to imagine that all shags released have survived this ordeal. The birds that return are skinnier, with significantly less body fat, and can be identified as a result. Once they rejoin the group, however, these shags quickly return to the standard weight and shape, making it once again impossible to tell them apart from the rest. Among the flock, there must always be at least several birds that have been caught and subsequently released by factory personnel.

"BUT YOU KNOW WHAT I MEAN, RIGHT? HOW SHE TALKS. It's dark. Dark, or, what—closed off?" "Well, if she were more outgoing, she wouldn't be a 26-year-old contract worker, would she?" "I don't know. These days, it's not uncommon for young women to get into temp work. Lots of them are really hard-working, serious girls, too. There are only so many jobs out there, right? That's not what I mean, though. It's the way she talks. She can't communicate. If you don't make her talk, if you don't ask direct questions, she won't say anything. If you don't talk about something she wants to talk about, she'll just sit there. But as soon as you mention something that interests her, she starts going a million words a minute and doesn't even give you time to respond. That's not a conversation. I've always heard that young people are bad at communicating, but this is something else. If you're that closed off, there's no way you could pass an interview." "Yeah, maybe." "Some people are just quiet. They're not talkers. And that's fine. Your sister, though, once she gets going, you can't get her to shut up. She doesn't listen to anything anyone else says, but if you stop listening to her, she'll get all bent out of shape and go quiet again. All she does is complain. It'd be different if she wanted to tell you about her hobbies or her interests or something, but she's always so negative. How are you even supposed to respond to that? And she's frowning all the time, I really can't stand it. Sorry, I know I'm supposed to be a professional." A professional what? "It's fine. We're not really that close." "I don't know, you looked pretty close when we met. Sorry, are you mad at me? You are, aren't you?" "I'm not." "I'm sorry. Sorry, but, yeah, that's what I honestly thought. It's good she has a job now. If she messes this one up, I guess she could register with us, but I'm not so confident that I could place her somewhere." "No, she's fine. I actually think this job's a good fit for her. She doesn't have to talk and it's full-time, even if the pay isn't great ... Hey, I didn't realize you were interviewing her." "Occupational hazard." Listening to my brother and his girlfriend talk in an American coffee shop inside the factory, I learned that my brother had lost his job in computers and was working as a temp for his girlfriend's agency. They couldn't see me, but from where I was sitting, hidden behind a potted snake plant, I had a decent view of her. Her hair was shorter now. My brother had his back to me, but I could tell he was wearing the gray shirt I'd ironed for him the night before. I'd ordered coffee with whipped cream, but by the time I tried to take a sip, the cream had already melted, and I was left with a normal bitter cafe au lait. I thought about sweetening it, but didn't know where to find the sugar. I didn't want to get up and make a fool of myself. Not again. After I'd placed my order, I stood in the wrong place. It was mortifying. "Miss, could I ask you to wait over here?" "The job's okay, I think. I'm getting the hang of it, but I don't know how to tell my sister. I mean, contract work is better than temp work, right?" "There's no better or worse. You're making good money and you're bound to get a raise at some point. You just have to stick with it. All the girls we placed here said they got a lot out of it. That's why I wanted you here." "I appreciate it. It's just a completely different field." "You'll get used to it. Try to keep an open mind. One step at a time." She was drinking something hot out of a ceramic cup. I already knew

88

what my brother was drinking, even though I couldn't see it—it was an iced coffee. He lives on iced coffee. If it's on the menu, that's what he gets. Why did she get a real cup? My drink came in some stupid paper cup. She put the cup down on her saucer with a clank. Then she picked up a small fork and stabbed into what appeared to be a slice of cheesecake. They serve dessert here? Maybe she ordered it off some special menu. I never come to cafés like this. They make me nervous. But I have a right to be here. My brother was stirring the ice in his glass. "It takes way more out of me than working with computers. I can't stay focused. It kills my eyes, too." "Are you kidding? It's got to be easier on your eyes than staring at a screen all day." What kind of work is he doing? It has to be something at the factory. Why else would they be meeting here? I felt bad for him, starting over at thirty, in something apparently unrelated to computers. He should have told me. He should have told me he was working here. I'm sure he didn't know what to say. I'm sure he was embarrassed. But I'm his sister. We live together. How did he think I was going to react? That night, he didn't come home. There wasn't anything out of the ordinary about that, not really, but I felt terrible. I couldn't sleep. I wanted her to die. I wanted them to break up. I replayed in my head all the things she said to him about me, about his little sister. Who the hell does that? Someone so hopelessly imbecilic should do everyone a favor and just die. What the hell is wrong with the world? To think that a first-rate idiot like that can be gainfully employed, while me and my brother, good and humble citizens, are disenfranchised, unable to find permanent work. I curled up in a ball and whispered *die, die, die* until I finally fell asleep. In the morning, I could barely wake up. I wasn't ready for work. I wasn't ready for the world. I was hoping for a natural disaster, but it was a beautiful day. I forced myself out of bed and went to work.

My head wasn't in it. Even if it wasn't, so what? My job couldn't be any simpler. (Thinking about it, it's really insane that the factory pays me as much as they do. Why not automate the process?) The more my thoughts wander the harder it gets—everything feels so disconnected. Me and my work, me and the factory, me and society. There's always something in the way. It's like we're touching, but we're not. What am I doing here? I've been living on this planet for more than twenty years, and I still can't talk properly, can't do anything that a machine can't do better. I'm not even operating the shredder. I'm only assisting it. I guess I'm working, but it actually feels like I'm getting paid money I don't deserve, like I'm surviving on money I haven't earned. It didn't feel like time was moving, but the clock on the wall said I'd been at work for three hours. Just then, Goto snuck up behind me. "Hey, Ushiyama-san, you haven't used any vacation time since you got here. We're really cracking down on that, so be sure you take your days off, okay? Full-time employees get three days off after six months. You can roll over the days you don't use, but it's best if you use them. In fact, take the rest of today off. Why don't you go home now?" He was right behind me, and now he was practically pushing me out the door—I didn't even see him coming until he was right in my face. He always looked a little drunk, but today he looked even worse. I doubt I looked any better. I really wasn't myself. I was sleep-deprived and agitated. I had no desire to be here. Still, it didn't occur to me to take time off until Goto suggested it. I didn't even know that was a possibility. No one had ever mentioned it. Not Itsumi, not the Captain, nobody. Now Goto was here, pretty much telling me I was ruining things by working all the time. I only heard: "We'll be okay without you, just leave." Feeling like the best thing I could do was comply, I feebly said, "Fine." If I didn't go now, I'd have to track down Goto some other time anyway. I just wanted to get it over with. "Okay. In that case, you'll need to fill out the form. Sign and date it, get Samukawa-san to stamp it, then bring it over to me. The forms should be in there," Goto said, pointing at a cabinet in the shredder station. He rolled his shoulders as he walked off. I bet he's hitting the links with the higher-ups on his days off. Maybe that's his strategy for getting ahead in the factory, but he should probably give a little more thought to his physical appearance. Don't walk around looking like a drunk all the time. I searched the drawer that Goto had pointed to, but found only a brittle rubber thimblette and a staple remover. I looked through the others, one at a time. In the bottom drawer, I found a shallow cardboard box containing A6-size sheets with PAID VACATION REQUEST FORM written on the top. Never knew these were here. Itsumi had never mentioned them. Being told I could go home in the middle of the day was not entirely disappointing. Still, I couldn't help feeling disappointed. If I'd known this was possible, I wouldn't have come in the first place. I put myself through hell to get out of bed. Still, if I can go home, I should go home. Just go. At the same time, I figured, well, I'm already here, why not walk around the factory for a little while to calm down. I didn't want to rush back to a house that smells like my brother, where I'd probably zone out in front of the TV and battle with my own demons for the rest of the day. In moments like this, you have to move around a little. Besides, no one would care if I walked around the factory during business hours, as long as I had my badge. I wasn't going to wander through the other buildings or anything. I'd stay outside, look at the trees and hills. The factory actually had a lot of green, and I thought I'd better try taking it in at least once, because who knows when I might quit. And if I did, I know I'd never come back.

I filled out the sheet, then took it over to the Captain, who'd just gotten to work. He had his reading glasses on, and was poring over some file open on his desk. When I cleared my throat, he looked up and removed his glasses. I explained the situation and handed him the sheet. He said something like *Ho-hoh*, then put the file away. "The managers had a meeting this morning. I bet Goto-san got an earful. 'You better be giving PTO to your contract workers,' or something like that." Well, that explains it. "Do you know what you're going to do with the rest of your day?" I told him I was thinking about walking around for a while. *Ho-hoh*, again, this time with a huge grin. "I've been here so long that there's really nothing left to see, but for someone like you exploring could be pretty interesting. Ushiyama-san, do you know about the river? The big one that goes to the ocean?" I was pretty sure I'd heard about it, but couldn't say for sure. "You've never seen it, have you? Well, there's a big bridge that runs between the north and south zones. The two sides couldn't feel more different. Everything over there is more, uh, physical. The buildings here are so metaphysical. Know what I mean? The bridge is beautiful, by the way. It was designed by some famous architect. You should go and take a look. There's no need to walk across it. Going the whole way is a real workout. But there's a bus that stops on the bridge. Maybe you could walk partway, then catch a bus—it's one of those free shuttles that circles around the factory. Anyway, you might like the view. From the bridge, you can see a lot of birds." I couldn't care less about bird-watching, but I decided to walk in that direction. It'd be nice to walk with a goal in mind. On my walk over, I saw lots of people dressed much more casually than I was. A few men lugging giant blocks of metal were wearing grungy gray jumpsuits that had been stained black with oil or ink. Other people were wearing suits, but most of them were in cars or on buses. When they were on foot, they would walk to the nearest bus stop and wait for a ride. Office girls were walking around in groups, holding clutches. There were some young women and men with their jackets off, playing a rowdy game of volleyball. Lunchtime aboveground was a beautiful thing. Everyone was wearing a badge. A lot of them had red straps, same as me, but I might have been the only red around without a jumpsuit on. "Permanent employees from HQ are dark blue, and the top dogs are black, but the top top dogs are silver. If you ask me, it looks more like gray than silver. Anyway, if you're silver you can basically go anywhere you want. In other words, silvers are the highest up. Executives or their heirs. Then there are the permanents from affiliates and subsidiaries. They're blue. Visitors get dark red, almost reddish-brown. Nonpermanents are always bright colors. Red, yellow, or shocking pink. There are supposed to be differences between them, probably related to the type of work. Physical labor, desk work, and so on." "Why do the nonpermanents get stuck with the colors that stand out?" "Well, most nonpermanent workers do physical work, right? If they keep their straps out while they're working, it can get kind of dangerous, like when you're using the shredder. You have to do something with the badge, take it off or something, right? Red and yellow are safety colors, aren't they? What color are you, Yoshiko-chan?" Red. What color's my brother? Yellow? Pink? "Just follow the signs that say TO SOUTH. They'll get you to the bridge. If you follow the main route, you can get on the bus if you get tired. There was a time when I used to walk all the way across that bridge to stay in shape, over and back, north and south." North and south? Come on, really, I thought, but when I got there, it really did feel that way. The river was so wide that you couldn't see the other bank from the foot of the bridge. It felt funny. Here I was, a single cog, a disposable laborer who'd never had the chance to experience the sheer size of the factory—the idea of crossing this huge bridge felt a little overwhelming. Am I really allowed to be here? I stopped and stared at the bridge. It was gigantic. Still, I'm not so sure you could call it beautiful. There were a few other pedestrians. A bus full of people in suits was coming over from the other side. The passengers must have been from the north, from HQ. They'd probably gone to the south zone for some meeting.

"Honestly, with the work we do in the Shredder Squad, I think we'd be more at home over there, in the south. Well, you'll see what I mean."

I stood there, unsure if I wanted to step onto the bridge. I could always turn around, or take the bus like the Captain said. If I made it all the way across, I could just leave the factory through the south gate. I didn't feel at all worn out from the walk to the bridge. I was sure it was going to take hours to get there, but it was still lunch. This river, this bridge, this factory. It was all so big, and I was a part of it—it had a space for me, a need for me. I should be grateful, right? Sure, it's a job that anybody could do—even an old man or a guy with a bad leg. In that sense, maybe it's not the best place for a young woman with her whole life ahead of her. Still, most people my age are holed up in their rooms with nothing to do. I want to work, and I'm lucky enough to be able to. Of course I'm grateful for that. How could I not be? Except, well, I don't want to work. I really don't. Life has nothing to do with work and work has no real bearing on life. I used to think they were connected, but now I can see there's just no way. If I tried explaining that to Itsumi, she'd say something like she did at yakiniku, about how you have to keep on fighting. But that's not the point. I've worked my whole life, and it's never been a fight, not at all. It's always been stranger than that, harder to grasp. It's not even something inside of me. It's out there, out in the world. How could I ever control that? I thought I'd been giving it everything I had, but what I thought was my everything had no real value. Just look at the way I am now. That's proof. I don't want to work. I don't, but what else am I doing with my life? Clearly walking wasn't helping. If anything, I was sinking, with each step, deeper into my own thoughts. I kicked one leg in front of the other, kept on going. Maybe I should've just gone home and watched reruns. Whatever—even if it doesn't bring me any pleasure, at least I'm making some sort of living. I've been fortunate. Beyond blessed. I have to accept that. So what if there's something in the way? I'm sure work is like that for everyone. I can't always act like a spoiled child. Thoughts racing through my head, I stopped where I was. I couldn't see the end of the bridge, ahead or behind me. How far had I come? How long had I been walking? Looking over the side, there was nothing but water. Is this the ocean? I thought the bridge ran straight across the river, but maybe it actually ran over it, right down the middle. Where's the shore? The walkway was fairly wide, but with every vehicle that rushed by, I got hit with another gust of wind. Most of the cars were silver sedans with factory logos on the door, but there were also a few black or red hatchbacks and some giant wagons that looked like American imports. Whenever a bus came, it would stop on the bridge and let a couple of people off. One of the buses waited for me, assuming I wanted a ride, but I waved to the driver to let him know I wasn't getting on. The bus sped ahead, leaving a cloud of black smoke in its wake. The buses on the bridge came in various colors and patterns, some that I'd never seen before. Were they using old buses they'd bought from other bus companies? Everybody who got off was wearing a gray jumpsuit. They made their way toward a series of ladders that led up and down from the bridge. They pulled out their keys to unlock the cages at the base of the ladders, then passed what were probably tools to men above and below them. If I'd looked up, I'm sure I would have seen more men in gray jumpsuits, but I didn't dare. I was scared, so I turned away. I grabbed hold of the railing and looked down into the water. I couldn't tell which way the current was moving. I thought I could feel the water pulling me down. I'd never been good with heights. I felt like I wanted to fall in, so I took a few steps back. I started to worry that I'd lost track of which side of the bridge I'd come from, but the cars beside me were still heading in the same direction. No way I could have gotten spun around. The cars were constant, speeding by with unrelenting force. I started walking again, figuring I'd get on the bus at the next stop. I still hadn't eaten lunch. I had something in my bag, but I wasn't really in the mood. I just didn't feel hungry. Starting tomorrow, I'd better pack a lunch for my brother, too. How long had he been working at the factory anyway?

I'D NEVER SEEN SO MANY PEOPLE ON THE BRIDGE. WORK-
ers were moving up and down the ladders, and when I looked
over the side I could see even more of them below, by the river.
I'd seen men on the ladders before, but never like this. It's weird
to see so many people moving around overhead. They had to
be tethered to something, but I couldn't see any wires or ropes
from where I was standing. Did they actually climb all the way
up there? The spot with the black birds was a short walk away, a
little closer to the ocean. A breeze was blowing. It felt good. Un-
surprisingly, I didn't feel like reading that kid's report. First of
all, could a grade-schooler really type something like that? I bet
the old man had written it, and he was just using his grandson to
get me to read it. But why? As I walked on, I could hear the birds.
Is this what they sounded like? Did they always sound so sad?
Soon they came into view. "You have it? The A-pipe. The A . . ."
"Yeah, I got it." I could hear the men shouting. They probably
had to raise their voices to hear each other over the wind and
cars. I looked back, then looked ahead again. There were men all
over the bridge, spaced out at regular intervals. I bet they were
on the underside of the bridge, too. Every now and then, they
would yell and wave their arms. The sky was blue, with only an
occasional cloud speeding past, turning the world dark for a moment or two. I could see a woman on the bridge with both hands

on the railing, looking over the edge. She wasn't in uniform, just jeans and an old gray shirt, meaning she probably wasn't with the workers. I guess it's not too uncommon for people from the factory to walk across the bridge, but I'd never seen anyone stop halfway and stare over the side. For a second, I thought she might be considering suicide. But that didn't make any sense. There were men all around who would come to her rescue. We glanced at each other, then she did a double take, as if she recognized me. The closer I got to her, the younger she seemed. A little scary, though. Her cheeks drooped like a bulldog's. She had no makeup on and her eyebrows were so thin that they almost didn't exist. The birds were crying louder now, in their usual huddle, staring at the factory. I can't go down to the bottom today, I told myself. The men on the bridge would stop me. Still, I had my camera, and I wasn't going to let the opportunity go to waste. I took the camera out of its case and pointed it at the birds. I zoomed in and took a shot, but when I saw the image on the LCD display, the birds didn't look like themselves. The damp sheen had vanished from their wings. I knew this camera had its limitations, but the results were far worse than expected. It hadn't occurred to me to pack any special lenses, either. My best telephoto lens was too heavy to carry this far anyway. I decided to make do with what I had. I'd have to get closer and wait for one to leave the group. The moment I saw one fly up, I took aim—as if I had the skill necessary to shoot a bird in flight. When the bird landed on the water, I followed it, taking a couple of steps toward the railing with the viewfinder pressed against my eye. After I had a few shots, I lowered the camera and saw the woman I'd passed earlier. She was glaring at me now. She looked a lot older than before. Her eyes were narrowed, and the wrinkles on her bulldog face were taut. She probably thought I was trying to take her picture. She spun around, like she was about to storm off. Maybe she thought I was some kind of pervert, like the guy in the forest. I thought I should tell her what I was doing, that it was all a big misunderstanding. I started to run after her. When she saw me coming, though, her scowl deepened. Chasing after her probably wasn't helping. Now I really had to apologize. "Sorry," I said, watching the anger on her face give way to terror. Once I was close, I could see that she really was young. "I'm sorry, I wasn't taking your picture. It probably looked that way, but I'm pretty sure you weren't in the frame. Anyway, I was shooting the birds. You looked, uh, worried, so I thought ..." She muttered something and nodded skeptically. I couldn't tell if she was looking at me or not. Then she bowed and said, "I'm sorry ..." Wait, why was she apologizing? What was I supposed to say? I was the one who started this conversation, so I'd better finish it, I thought, but before I could find the right words, she asked, "You were taking pictures of those birds?" Those birds? "Y-yeah," I answered, taken aback. "Do you know what they're called?" Why does she want to know? Why does everyone want to know about these birds?

I COULD SEE THEIR WINGS. NORMAL-LOOKING BLACK WA-
terfowl. They had funny cries, though. Maybe they were cat
gulls. But do we get cat gulls this far south? I kept walking. As
the river widened, it started to smell like the ocean, and I found
a lot more birds. They were crowded together, maybe twenty or
thirty of them. What were they doing? Protecting their chicks,
maybe? On the nature channel, I'd seen penguins doing the same
thing, to keep warm in the winter. Were they cold? I stopped
and leaned over the railing to get a better look, catching a nose-
ful of bird smell, thick and greasy, together with the sea breeze.
Were these the birds the Captain was talking about? They were
average in every way. They weren't especially big or small, just
solid black from beak to tail. Their wings glistened in the sun.
The only thing even remotely interesting about them was their
numbers. I looked around. How close was the southern end of
the bridge? At this point, it made more sense to walk all the way
across. But now that I'd stopped to look at the birds, my legs felt
heavy. Clouds were forming in the sky, cars were rushing past.
The birds were all facing the same direction, squawking over
one another. A middle-aged man was walking along the bridge
after me. He wasn't in a suit, but was reasonably well-dressed.
He was wearing glasses and a collared shirt, a bulky black bag
slung over his shoulder. He was pale, almost skeletal. As he got

closer, I could see a gray strap around his neck. Gray? No, it was silver. Top-level clearance. Is that even possible? He was only in his forties, maybe younger. Our eyes met for a moment before he walked past me. Who was this guy? He was restless, looking up and down, in all directions. From behind, he looked a little hunched over. I guess there are all sorts of people in the factory. But he didn't look like an executive. Maybe his dad was some bigshot. That would explain the color of his strap, at least. If that's the case, I told myself, I'd better keep my distance. I went back to looking at the birds. The Captain said he used to cross this bridge all the time, but I just couldn't imagine how. Maybe if he took a really long lunch. What time was it anyway? It was hard to believe that all this was the property of a single company. I decided I'd keep going, to the end of the bridge, but when I looked up, the man with the silver strap was pointing his camera in my direction. What the hell's he doing? I don't care what color his badge is, he doesn't have the right to take my picture. Why would he even want to? I don't know, maybe he was aiming at something else and I was just in the way. That was far more likely. It's not like I'm particularly beautiful, or even cute. Then again, it's a crazy world we live in. I'm sure plenty of men out there are really into plain-looking factory girls. But, no, that wasn't it. Maybe he thought I was misbehaving or breaking some kind of rule and was taking my picture as evidence. Proof that I was skipping work or looking at something I wasn't supposed to see. People don't typically cross this bridge on foot, so he probably thought I was up to something. But, no, wait. He was the one who was up to something. Something creepy. Okay, I was probably letting my imagination get the best of me. Maybe he just wanted a photo of the factory from the bridge. Whatever the case, I thought, I should head back the way I came. I mean, what other choice did I have? Even if he was taking pictures of me, what could I say to make him stop? I didn't have the words.

I turned around to leave, but I saw him out of the corner of my eye, rushing toward me. He was moving faster now, practically sprinting—but what could I do? I couldn't outrun him. And what would be the point? There were men all around us, working on the bridge, and a steady flow of cars and buses only a few feet away. I was safe here. The man ran up to me, but I was frozen in place, unable to move. The short run had left him winded, and once he caught his breath he lowered his head in apology. "I'm sorry, I wasn't taking your picture. It probably looked that way, but I'm pretty sure you weren't in the frame. Anyway, I was shooting the birds. You looked, uh, worried, so I thought ..." I nodded. That made sense. He wasn't taking my picture after all. I was just in the way. I was kind of relieved, but also a little confused. What was it about these birds? "I'm sorry," I said. "You were taking pictures of those birds?" I pointed my finger at the black splotch in the distance. "Y-yeah, those," he bleated, nodding excessively. I hesitated, then asked, "Do you know what they're called?" For a couple of seconds, he just stared at me blankly. Did he even understand what I was saying? "Why would you ask me that?" "Huh?"

"These pickles are really something," Furufue said. We were right in the middle of our soki soba when the owner, who had brought us our bowls maybe a minute earlier, suddenly roared: "Okay, everyone. I count ten customers now, and you know what that means! It's time for our sata andagi showdown!" I looked around the room. The three other groups were getting excited, as if they knew what was going to happen next. "Okay. get ready for it." The others all held out their right hands. Furufue and I looked at each other, confused. The owner turned to the two of us and said, "Come on, folks. This is handmade sata andagi we're talking about. You won't want to pass this up." I had zero interest, but couldn't see an easy way out. I made a fist, and Furufue did the same. "Okay, here we go. Rock, paper, shisa!" Shisa? I kept my fist in a ball. Rock. I was lucky enough to get knocked out in the first round. Furufue was less lucky. His paper kept him in the game. "What luck you've all got. Okay, here we go again. Ready? Rock. Paaaper ... Shisa!" In the end, a young woman with black hair parted down the middle emerged the winner. She flexed her muscles in victory, claimed the plastic bag with three pieces of sata andagi inside, and promised one piece to the woman she'd come with. Having finally lost, Furufue turned his attention back to his bowl of soba. "Crap. It's cold," he said, gnawing on a spare rib.

"I think they're called factory shags, but I can't say for sure," he said, his expression dark. "Well, I'm sure that's not the official name." "You never looked it up? Factory shag?" I asked. "I only heard the name for the first time this morning, actually." The wind picked up all of a sudden. Workers above us were shouting. I looked around, worried that a stray tool or screw might come flying toward us, but after one hard gust, the wind subsided. "I think they're related to cormorants. But I looked into it a little, and they really aren't like other cormorants. This one's black all over. The river and ocean cormorants we have in Japan are never black around the eyes. Their beaks are always yellow. I wanted a better look, so I brought my camera to get some pictures." "Where'd you hear that they're called factory shags?" "An old man and his grandson came to my house this morning." "An old man and his grandson?" "They took part in a moss hunt I led." Moss hunt? Is this guy for real? What's he talking about? "Well, that's why I'm here. What about you? Are you on your lunch break?" What was I doing here? I should have run for the bus. "I took the afternoon off. I'm heading home now. The factory's so big, though, I thought I might as well take a walk around. Then my team leader suggested checking out the bridge. He said it was a beautiful place with lots of birds. So I came." When I tried to explain, it came out sounding ridiculous. To begin with, why am

I taking time off if I'm not even leaving the factory? Are they really going to count this as paid time off? I know I punched out when I left the building, but what if there was some sort of error? More importantly, why did I come all this way to see an unremarkable bridge and some stupid black birds? Because the Captain said so? I don't have a clear enough map of the factory to say for sure, but I probably came a long way. "Oh, okay. I see," the man said, nodding. "So you just came for a quick look. You're not really interested in the birds. In that case, my apologies. And please don't worry about the photos. You weren't in them." The man bowed and hurried off. I nodded back, but didn't have time to say anything else. I stood there for a moment, then decided to keep going. I was getting hungry now, but still didn't feel like eating what I'd brought for lunch—just some fried frozen food and rice I'd cooked the night before. If there weren't so many people working on the bridge, I probably would have tossed the whole thing into the water right there. Since we were headed in the same direction, I wanted to give the man a head start, so it wouldn't look like I was trying to follow him. I managed to kill a little time just leaning against the railing, looking at the birds and the men working around the bridge, and when the man with the camera was basically a stick figure in the distance, I started moving again. I'll get on the bus at the next stop, I told myself, but I reached the end of the bridge before I found one. I hadn't even been walking that long. I couldn't see how I'd already made it across, but there I was. How could I have made it this far in so little time? I must've made it most of the way before I'd stopped to look at the birds. It was kind of disappointing. I turned around and there he was again, right there. I know that I stare at the ground when I walk, but how did I fail to see him until I got this close? He was standing in front of an Okinawan restaurant with a red banner and a couple of lion-faced shisa statues standing guard. He was too busy studying the building to notice me. This could be awkward. I was about to slip away, when I caught myself muttering, "Oh, um ..." Turning toward me, the man raised his eyebrows in surprise. "Did you need something?" *Did you need something?* What kind of response is that? "I'm just going home." "Well, take care. And sorry about earlier," he said, lowering his head again. I tried to leave quickly, but for some reason my feet wouldn't move. He looked at me, then at the restaurant's sign. After a couple of moments, he asked, "Hey, um, did you know this was here?" What is this supposed to be? Small talk? "No. This is my first time across the bridge ..." I'm pretty sure I'd already told him that earlier, but maybe he'd forgotten. Maybe it was the wind, but all his hair was pushed to one side. "Right, right. Sorry. It's just, I've never seen this here, and it doesn't look new. I'm always walking around the factory. I know the area pretty well, so ..." All of a sudden he was Mister Talkative. What was going on here? After showing no interest, even being downright rude, why was he so chatty now? Wait. I'm a young woman, talking to a middle-aged man. How could I let this happen? He's probably into me. What if this is his way of asking me to lunch? After all, we're standing in front of this restaurant, during lunch, talking about the place. Is he trying to say: "How about we go inside?" I felt like I was sweating. Was I? I thought I could smell it. "Well, it's all new to me, honestly." "It's odd, though. Maybe I'm getting senile." I bet he just wants to spend some time with a young woman, any young woman. If that's true, I'd better be on guard. I couldn't bear the silence any longer, so I asked, "Have you eaten?" "Lunch? Not yet." "Me neither," I replied. More silence. There was only a faint hiss coming from somewhere, from the factory, or the birds, or maybe from inside the restaurant. After some time, he asked, "Well, how about we eat together?" Well ... "Why not." For a second, I was nervous he thought I'd been angling for an invite, but he just nodded, then we went inside. I'd never set foot in any of the cafeterias or restaurants around the factory. Was this even okay? There's not going to be some problem when I go to pay or something? What if I have to be a permanent employee? What if they check my strap? Even if that doesn't happen, what if nonpermanent workers have to pay extra? It seemed reasonable to expect the man to pay, but would he? "Come on in," said the owner. He had a mustache and an indigo-dyed cloth wrapped around his head. "Sit anywhere you like." But most of the seats were taken. There were three groups already eating, eight customers total. It was down to one open table and a couple of spaces at the counter. The other customers were smiling, laughing, apparently enjoying their meals. This was my first time in an Okinawan restaurant, and my first time eating out with a man other than my brother—even if it was some random middle-aged guy. We went to the table and sat down. "We're still serving lunch, if you're interested," the owner said, placing a pair of heavy-bottomed tumblers full of water in front of us. Looking over the handwritten menu, I was almost happy. *Lunch Specials: Soki Soba Set—Goya Champloo Set—Tempura Set (Squid and Seasonal Fish)—Daily Special. Sets may include: vegetables, rice, noodles, miso soup.* "The special today is fuirichi, with a side of rafute." "I think I'll go with the soki soba, just on its own," said the man with the silver strap. I'd been thinking about the daily special, but the man I was with ordered a single bowl of noodles. That being the case, he'd be done long before I could finish everything. As a woman, it just didn't feel okay. "I'll have the same, thanks," I said. The owner nodded and took off. On its own, the soba is 150 yen cheaper than the set. If the set doesn't come with rice and miso soup (maybe it does, it's impossible to tell from the menu), if it just comes with boiled vegetables or something, then avoiding the set makes a lot of sense. From where I was sitting, I couldn't really see the other diners. What were they eating? "By the way, I'm Furufue." Furufue? There's a name you don't hear too often. He started talking. I'd been reading the menu, to keep myself entertained, but put it down when he started to talk. "I'm Ushiyama." "Ushiyama-san. Where do you work? What do you do?" he asked. "Thanks for waiting. Here you go, two bowls of soki-i-i soba." "I work with shredders, destroying documents." "I see. Well, let's eat before it gets cold." "Yeah, okay." I looked inside my bowl. Thick yellow noodles and pork in a clear, almost colorless broth. Green onions and pink pickles on top. "Hey, this is pretty good." "Yeah, it is. Seriously, though, I love my job. Shredding really unleashes the artist in me." Furufue didn't laugh at my joke. He just looked confused, so I stopped talking and went back to my soba.

"WELL THEN, FURUFUE-SAN, CAN I ASK YOU ABOUT THAT project? What exactly have you been doing? It's been fifteen years, right? In that time, what have you accomplished? You haven't just been leading the moss hunt this entire time, have you? It seems pretty clear that the factory turned to someone else to green the roofs and walls. It looks like the whole thing was outsourced, but who knows. I suppose that doesn't match up with what you were told when you started here. I just can't understand it, though ... It doesn't make any sense to put one person in charge of greening all the buildings for the whole complex. Just like you said, how would you even know where to start with a project that size? Still, in terms of your accomplishments so far, to tell you the truth, I don't see anything. Am I off base here? Surely you must have done something ... You should have been able to do something ..." Maybe Aoyama was right. Talking with that young woman at the Okinawan restaurant and trying to explain what I do, even I was struck by the strangeness of it all. "What's the connection between moss and the factory? What did that job description look like?" When I told her that my advisor recommended me for the job, then practically forced me to take it, she bared her front teeth and wrinkled her face in judgment. "You're paid a monthly salary?" As soon as she asked, her expression relaxed and she added, "I'm sorry, it's none of my business." I knew I shouldn't tell her how much I make, but I couldn't see anything wrong with telling her that I get paid the same amount on a monthly basis. When I said this, she nodded and said, "Yeah, thought so." But if I told her how much, I'm sure her face would tighten back up again. Sometimes, when I'm watching the news and I hear what salarymen are making, the figure's so low I can barely believe it. But since it's television, they're probably making it sound worse than it really is. Still, I get the feeling that I make more than average. Aoyama had hinted as much on occasion, and when Goto switched departments he said so to my face. "People don't get raises year after year. Not these days. The same goes for factory employees. That's the age we live in. Or maybe it's just me. But look at you, Furufue-san. All that time you spent as a researcher in college really paid off. Well, not that I know how much you make or anything." They give me a place to live, and the rent subtracted from my salary is just 9,000 yen per month—in other words, far, far below average. I don't own a car, and nothing else in my life really costs money. I'm sure it's more expensive to eat in the cafeterias and restaurants around the factory than it would be to cook at home, but even that doesn't cost me very much. My mother's always sending me care packages and I don't have any real hobbies, so my savings keep growing without any real effort on my part. I'd be fine without an annual raise, or the biannual bonuses, but could I actually say that to the factory? What good would come from complaining about getting paid this much for doing nothing? If I told my superiors thanks but no thanks? I live quietly, read about the world of bryology online, and grow shiso and cherry tomatoes in my backyard garden. I've even thought about buying a small dog a couple of times. This is my life. This is what I'm paid to do. And what's wrong with that? It's not like if I refused to take my salary it would somehow find its way to the people struggling to make ends meet. No point getting caught up in some unnecessary conflict. "How many years have you been doing this now? Collecting and studying moss." Fifteen, going on sixteen. And every day during that time, I'd been working. Not once had I actually stayed at home and just spent the day relaxing. I'm pretty sure I was doing what the factory wanted. They came to me with the bizarre task of green-roofing the entire factory on my own, then told me to take whatever time I needed. They can't complain. "The original job offer was related to green-roofing, but nothing's really come out of that." "Oh, that's moss? I thought it was just grass." What was she talking about? "At first, the factory seemed gray to me, but some of the roofs and walls are actually green." What? "I've seen lots of buildings like that around. So that was you?" It wasn't me. "I bet it was contractors. It had to be. You know this, but the vegetation around the factory isn't even our territory. That's General Affairs, or the Center for Corporate Social Responsibility, if it's about the environment or protecting the environment. In the PR Department, all we ask is that you run the Family Moss Hunt," Aoyama said. Even over the phone, I could imagine her smile, which had become a little more strained following her brief marriage. "I don't know what Goto-san told you, but my responsibilities with you don't go beyond the hunt. That's it." She never called him *Goto-san* when they were working in the same office. Now she made no effort to hide the fact that Goto belonged to another department. "Do you want me to confirm that?" "With whom?" "With CCSR or GA, whoever's in charge of green-roofing. All we have to do is ask. We can track down the contractors, too." But I really don't care who did it. That's not why I called. What I want to know is why I'm here. If they don't need me, then why am I here? "Do you want me to get in touch with Goto-san?" Aoyama was clearly annoyed. No, she wasn't the sort of person to show her emotions to someone who wasn't very close, so I probably had it wrong. Actually, talking to Goto made the most sense. It was probably the most appropriate course of action, but it still didn't feel right. He and I had never really gotten along, and I doubted he wanted anything to do with me now. Where did he even end up? "He's in the factory. Closer to HQ. In a different department. It's perfectly normal for people to transfer between departments. It happens all the time." Aoyama sighed into the receiver. "I'll reach out again closer to the moss hunt. Also, how would you feel about running the hunt not just once but twice a year? Everybody loves it. It's something we should really think about, moving forward." "Well, I mean, I've been experimenting with moss, working on green-roofing, but there are some sticking points, technically speaking. Honestly, the project has always been more or less impossible. I've done everything I can, it just hasn't led me anywhere." "Furufue-san, how long have you been working here?" "Fifteen years." "And during those years, have you produced anything? Anything tangible?" When I hung up, I felt this tension—knots—in my neck and my back. I rolled my shoulder blades a few times, then picked up the binder that the old man and his grandson had given me. As I started reading, I felt something funny on my lip. When I touched my face, it tickled my fingers. I guess I had a little bit of a beard going. I was stunned, but only for a fraction of a second. It wasn't anything, after all. Hair had been growing everywhere, on the backs of my hands, all over my body.

I WOKE UP AGAIN. I WAS DRENCHED IN SWEAT. WHAT WAS I reading? I couldn't find any typos or mistakes. And without additional instructions I couldn't do anything about the style. What was this supposed to be anyway? It didn't seem like the sort of thing that would need proofreading. It was almost like some kid's school project—except it was completely made up. True, there's a big river that cuts through the factory, and I'm sure we have some cleaning facilities, too, but the rest of it has nothing to do with reality. Shags and lizards? Lizards can't survive on lint. They eat bugs. In warmer places, there are larger lizards that feed on animals, but tiny ones that eat soap? The same goes for shags that can only be found in the factory. And why the hell would workers want to capture birds like that? It was nonsense, of course, but here it was on my desk. I had to do something with it, but what? Pull out my red pen and make edits? How? After a little thought, I returned the folder to its packet and threw it back where it came from. It's not like we have to handle these documents in any order anyway. Someone else can deal with it. I almost read the whole stupid thing, though. At least I think I did. They always make me read things that put me to sleep.

IT WAS RAINING THE MORNING AFTER I HAD LUNCH WITH Furufue, the middle-aged man with the silver ID strap. (I double-checked. It was silver. Academics are idolized—even when they're studying moss.) Walking in from the rain, I ran into Goto. "Good morning." "Morning." I thought about saying thanks for giving me the afternoon off, but he was clearly in a hurry, pinching an unlit cigarette, anxious to get outside. Getting to the smoking area multiple times a day had to be a lot of work. Inside, Hanzake was doing the same morning stretches as always. The Giant was there, too, playing around with a Muscle Man eraser. "Morning." "Good morning." "It's really coming down." "Yeah it is." I put my apron on, sat down, and opened my book. Every time somebody came through the door, the smell of rain filled the room. When the Captain came in, he said hello to Hanzake and me. He took his hat off and hung it on the Power Tower before opening a can of coffee he'd probably bought on the way in. "Ushiyama-san, how was the bridge?" "The bridge?" Hanzake perked up at the sound of the Captain's voice, craning what little neck he had to look at the Captain, then me, then the Captain again. "Ushiyama-san took the afternoon off, remember? She went for a walk around the factory," the Captain said, smiling at me. "You chose a good day for it." "I made it across the bridge. I saw the birds, too." I saw them, but they weren't anything special. They were just plain black birds, but somehow I felt like I had to report back. "There were a lot of them." "But it probably wasn't very interesting for you. They're just ordinary birds, after all. After you left, I started wondering if I shouldn't have said anything." "No, I had a good time. I'd never been over the bridge before. On the way there, I kept thinking about getting on a bus, but I ended up walking the whole way. Once I was on the south side, I caught the bus. I still can't believe how big the factory is." "You walked over the bridge? On foot?" Hanzake cut in, surprised. "I'd never make it." "It really is pretty far. I wonder how many miles. Ushiyama-san, how long did it take you?" "Not too long. Maybe a little over an hour? Under an hour and a half." On the other side, when we sat down at the Okinawan place, lunch was basically over, but they let us order off the lunch menu, so it had to be around two. It felt like I'd been walking longer than that. It really is a big bridge. You can't even see one end from the other. Why was it so easy to cross? "There were so many birds. I'd never seen anything like it." "I know, there are tons, right?" There really were. How do they all stay fed? "Still, you didn't get tired from the walk?" "It was fine." "What? You went for a walk?" Itsumi asked as she walked in, showing up at the last second as usual. "I hope you had good shoes on. Otherwise you can really mess up your knees and ankles," she said, putting her hair up in a bun. The usual melody played, and I could hear Goto calling the Print Services Branch Office morning meeting to order. As soon as we left the restaurant, Furufue and I parted ways. He took care of the check. When I thanked him, he laughed nervously and waved his hand in front of his face. He said he was going to walk around the factory before heading home, and I said I was going to take the bus. There was a stop right by the Okinawan place, and the bus came after a couple of minutes. In the south zone, all the buildings were squat and grimy with age. The trees were different, too. In the north zone, they're green with life all year round, but most of the trees in the south are yellow and dying, if not bare and dead. Some of them were giant, though, unlike any I'd ever seen. The flower beds had simple marigolds and scarlet sage. Most of the people I could see were wearing uniforms, but there was one woman with big earrings and high heels. As soon as she got on, a sweet smell filled the bus. Starting from the bridge, the bus hit every stop in the south zone before arriving at the south gate. The woman with the earrings got off at Processing Plant West. She thanked the driver as she carefully stepped onto the ground. Next came Processing Plant Central, Processing Plant East, Main Testing Site, then Warehouse X. At every stop, a couple of people got off and more people got on. Along the way, we were joined by a boy wearing shorts, an old man who looked far too old to work, and a housewife in an apron. A few kids with chunky backpacks got on, their spittly talk quickly spreading through the bus. An older man in a gray uniform asked the kids, "Half day?" No one answered him. The boys didn't even seem to notice. They got off before long, fortunately, but their tinny voices lingered behind. When we pulled up to the final stop, I thanked the driver and exited the bus. For a moment, I wasn't sure how to get to the gate, but most of the other passengers were walking briskly in the same direction, so I followed them. Soon I could see a fence and the glass-paned room where the security guard on duty was talking to somebody. Maybe you don't need to show your badge when you leave on this side. The guard gave me a slight nod as I walked past. I did the same. The soki soba wasn't very filling. I'd have to eat something else once I got home.

After the 9 a.m. chime, the rain only got heavier. When TRAN delivered the day's first haul of documents, the old paper gave off the usual dusty smell, only damper. Not long after, I walked upstairs to the bathroom, but it was closed for cleaning. It wasn't urgent, so I headed back down. On the way, I saw one of the overweight women coming up from the basement. Cradled in her pudgy arms was a black bird, just like the ones I'd seen at the river the day before. She had a tight grip on its wings, but it wasn't trying to fly away. It was definitely alive, surveying its surroundings. I stopped to watch, but the woman ignored me and kept walking up the stairs. Once she was past me, I turned around. Over her shoulders, I thought I could see black feathers. I couldn't do anything but stand there, listening to the rain getting louder whenever somebody opened the front door. What was she doing with that bird? If she was carrying it upstairs, it must have been in the basement, in the Print Services Branch Office. But where? It was dark in the stairwell—too dark for morning. When I finally regained the power to move, I made up my mind to ask Itsumi about the bird, but she was talking to one of the middle-aged women at the printing station. In the dark corner of the shredder station, a figure was sitting, reading a newspaper. Probably the Captain. Maybe it was Hanzake. The Giant was standing up straight, almost like the Captain's Power Tower, or maybe it really was the Power Tower, wearing the Captain's hat. I turned back toward the morning container, grabbed a handful of pages and fed them into the shredder. I wasn't thinking about anything at all, just feeding paper into the machine. Then, as soon as the shredder swallowed the last pages, I became a black bird. I could see people's legs, their arms. I saw gray, and a little green. I thought I could smell the ocean.